What the critics are saying:

"Vampire Fangs and Venom manages to combine vampires, werewolves, mythical beasts, aliens and time travel into one story. The presence of these diverse characteristics is well thought out and well explained. The life in Medieval England is described with enough detail to give the reader the flavor of the time period but not so much as to bog down the story." - Nicole LaFolle, Timeless Tales

"Richly crafted, detailed in every phrase, a stirring portrait of shapeshifting! If frolicking through the 14th century with a brilliant narrator as your guide is your cup of tea, buy a copy of Shifters' Desire: Vampire Fangs & Venom." – Connie, A Romance Review.

"Myra Nour writes stories that keeps you spell bound and this one is not exception!...Ms. Nour has written a very graphic story with love scenes that come together perfectly. They will heat your blood, ladies, you will need your fans handy. The characters are exciting and charming, and the passion in the characters just reach out to you." – Karen, Love Romances.

SHIFTER'S DESIRE
VAMPIRE FANGS & VENOM

by Myra Nour

SHIFTER'S DESIRE: VAMPIRE FANGS & VENOM
An Ellora' s Cave Publication, September 2004

Ellora' s Cave Publishing, Inc.
1337 Commerse Drive
Stow, Ohio 44224

ISBN #1-4199-5031-2

Shifter's Desire: Vampire Fangs & Venom © 2003 Myra Nour
MS Reader (LIT) ISBN # 1-84360-355-1
Mobipocket (PRC) ISBN # 1-84360-356-X
Other available formats (no ISBNs are assigned):
Adobe (PDF), Rocketbook (RB), Mobipocket (PRC) & HTML

Cover art by *Syneca*

Warning:

The following material contains graphic sexual content meant for mature readers. Shifter's Desire: Vampire Fangs & Venom has been rated E-rotic by a minimum of three independent reviewers.

Ellora's Cave Publishing offers three levels of Romantica™ reading entertainment: S (S-ensuous), E (E-rotic), and X (X-treme).

S-ensuous love scenes are explicit and leave nothing to the imagination.

E-rotic love scenes are explicit, leave nothing to the imagination, and are high in volume per the overall word count. In addition, some E-rated titles might contain fantasy material that some readers find objectionable, such as bondage, submission, same sex encounters, forced seductions, etc. E-rated titles are the most graphic titles we carry; it is common, for instance, for an author to use words such as "fucking", "cock", "pussy", etc., within their work of literature.

X-treme titles differ from E-rated titles only in plot premise and storyline execution. Unlike E-rated titles, stories designated with the letter X tend to contain controversial subject matter not for the faint of heart.

Also by Myra Nour:

As You Wish
Future Lost: *A Mermaid' s Longing*
Mystic Visions
Sex Kittens

SHIFTER'S DESIRE
VAMPIRE FANGS & VENOM

by Myra Nour

Chapter One

"Oh," she groaned aloud. There he was again, the dark mysterious figure that haunted her more nights than she cared to count. This time, they stood facing each other in the middle of a night-black forest; she was already frightened, her breathing frenzied and her heart pounding. She felt like she was caught in the middle of a *Twilight Zone* episode—death approached, but it was as if she were stuck in quagmire and couldn' t move.

He edged closer, stepped into the moonlit glade between her and the protective foliage that had covered his form. A werewolf! Briana was shocked. Even though she was a strong person, she was too scared to move an inch. She'd expected a menacing stranger, not a fictional monster. He looked real enough, his body bulky with muscles, and she even noticed a musky odor.

Abruptly, the creature jumped in one great predatory leap, landing directly in front of her. His weight crashed a small branch into kindling as he landed. Strangely, she wasn't frightened, not now. *Why?* She didn't know. Her heart thudded heavily against her chest, her breathing came out in short pants, but from another source entirely—she was turned on. Briana found this startling. The appearance of a savage, beast-like wolfman made her hot? It was insane, this sudden switch from terror to lust.

For years, she had been involved in strange encounters with this mystery man, who tonight, had turned out to be a nightmarish creature. But this was turning into the weirdest experience she'd ever had. Once he had made his appearance in wolf/human form, she no longer feared his presence. It was as if there was a connection between them, a hidden knowledge she found puzzling.

"Who are you?"

His answer was a guttural growl, then a pounce onto her body. She fell to the ground, landing uninjured on a soft pile of leaves. For some crazy reason, she knew he did not intend to hurt her. The beast's body was heavy, his long hair tickling against her exposed skin. She glanced down at her naked body, again surprised; she'd been wearing her nightgown earlier.

Drool dripped onto her chin and she looked up into its beautiful, but eerie golden eyes, strangely unaffected by the savage grin of its fanged mouth. She still wasn't frightened.

Suddenly, he swooped down on her neck, sucked up flesh into his mouth, his teeth delicately holding the skin, but not piercing it. His warm tongue licked between the fangs, up and down, then made swirls, as if he drew on an invisible artist' s palate. *My, it certainly felt real.*

Briana's insides churned, heat concentrated in her neck and connected with her lower body in a surprising rush. Moaning, she arched her back. She wanted...she didn't know what she wanted, perhaps more of his delicious feeling tongue. The werewolf released her with a quick flick of its tongue, then descended lower, nuzzled one breast, tickling the nipple into a hard nub simply with his downy soft facial hair. When he latched onto her nipple with his tongue and gentle nips of his teeth, her nerve endings were set to explode.

She could see nothing but his golden eyes; his body hair melded with the ink black night so efficiently. But she didn't need to see; she could feel. His large cock bumped against her thigh, as if asking permission to enter. Briana answered by spreading her legs wide, welcoming his hard length inside. She was ready, slick with need and wanting.

It was unbelievable…it felt so good. Felt like he belonged there always, moving his large body in a rhythm she matched stroke for stroke. Panting like an animal, she was as hot and horny as a bitch in heat. Gripping his hairy butt, she urged him forward faster and harder. His thick staff filled her completely and her vagina gripped him fiercely, squeezing her soft tissues in spasms around his hard length. An orgasm rippled through her and she moaned aloud.

Abruptly, she pitched into wakefulness in complete confusion. Where was she? For a second, Briana looked around for a hairy form, but only the interior of her cozy hotel room met her gaze. Stretching, she was startled by the dampness of her arousal and the aching throbbing that emitted in rhythmic beats from her cloth covered crotch. Pressing her hand against that erratic beat, Briana shuddered as another orgasm erupted. It was a slow, long lasting climax, which made her groan and push her hand into her lips harder. Biting her lower lip, she rode the last wave of sensation rippling through her clit.

Man, what a dream!

A wet dream! She knew this was common for men, but didn't think it was for women—she'd never experienced it before. Breathing slowly, she consciously slowed her body's response to the highly erotic dream. It took a few minutes, but finally she had control of herself again.

Why am I having such bizarre dreams when I' m having such a great time?

Briana not only didn't understand her strange, surreal dreams, but also didn't understand herself anymore—at least after last night. She was here in New Mexico on vacation, sequestered in a quiet spa resort, Los Ojos, enjoying her first true vacation in a long time.

The natural heated medicinal pools of the resort were heavenly; the soda pool was her favorite. She'd been soaking for hours each day. A daiquiri in hand made it easy to chat with others who came to relax as well. For the most part, the patrons of the spa were intellectuals, and like her, sought a quiet, less known place to relax. Briana had made several acquaintances, people she'd never see again, but it was surprising what you could discuss with strangers, private things you sometimes didn' t even share with friends. Subjects like dreams, goals unmet, and desires of the heart.

Exchanges about boyfriends and job issues made the rounds with little forethought. She realized that maybe the conversation and companionship were the biggest plus to her trip, not the hot springs "tubs", luxurious massages, pampering facial, nature hikes, or wonderful gourmet restaurant.

Briana was simply too busy as manager for a large hotel in Dallas to have much of a life, period. She didn't have regular girlfriends, unlike many of her co-workers; there never seemed to be time. She dated so infrequently it was the gossip of the hotel staff, and it was not due to her looks either; she was self-confident enough to know she looked just fine.

Not one of the men she'd ever dated had piqued her interest either for more than a short period of time. Again, she didn't understand why she seemed to have such a problem finding the right man. A few of the men had been "real catches", as the female staff would say. They had good jobs, their looks ranged from cute to downright handsome, and they drove luxury cars. Of course, being a modern woman, she didn't require a man to earn her living, and even orgasms could be easily achieved with a vibrator. But dates were nice. Having someone to share activities with was fun, and making love with a man was, for the most part, an experience she didn't want deleted from her life.

Lovemaking! Some lovers had been adequate, giving her an orgasm with mostly unskilled efforts, her climax probably due more to her own natural sensuality than anything else. A few were downright pitiful—a "two-minute man" wasn't for her!

Mark had come closest to someone she could spend a lifetime with. He was handsome and was the manager of a nearby hotel, so they had that in common. And they both enjoyed walks in the park, watching horror movies, and reading science fiction novels. He was even a spectacular lover, always bringing her to satisfaction more than once during a session.

But, there was something she couldn't put her finger on, some unfathomable reason why she couldn't commit. She wasn't afraid of commitment; at least she didn't think so. Mark had even asked in a diplomatic way about an engagement, which she'd ignored. He was the one who broke off their long-standing dating relationship, after she'd dragged her feet for months in giving him a response.

Getting up from the comfortable bed, she gulped down a glass of water. She had been having a fun vacation until *he* had appeared in her dreams. The dark figure she now knew was a wolfman. Sighing, she pushed the curtain aside, surprised when the sun's rays hit her full force. Dressing quickly, she thrust thoughts of her disturbing dream from her mind, determined to enjoy a full day of activities. And she did.

That night, she was exhausted. She'd made sure to hike, do yoga and swim, in order to guarantee a good night' s sleep. But, as she was drifting off peacefully, he called to her once again. She managed to ignore him and fall asleep anyway. Demanding attention, he made such a racket in her head; she finally awakened, disturbed and confused. She jumped up, grumpy and tired, but got dressed mechanically, without thinking.

She was restless, paced the floor for over an hour, and then suddenly decided to go for a drive. The road she chose was dark, much of it long and straight, stretching for miles with nothing breaking the boring landscape. Flatland, with ugly shrub brush frequently marred its surface. She must have driven for hours, her thoughts flitting back to him, and all the appearances he' d made into her night realm. At all times she' d been aware of him, as if he sat at the back of her mind and sang to her. It was eerie, but beautiful.

Finally, after hours, she pulled into some kind of cleared area. That singsong voice had stopped and somehow she knew she'd arrived at her destination. She was exhausted. Briana fell into a restless sleep. Waking at predawn, when the land was gray and indistinguishable, she waited for the sun to rise so she could see where the heck she'd driven herself during the night. She did not feel refreshed.

It was dusky dark, not much to see except the huge, dark hump of something big directly in front of her vehicle. Probably a mountain from its shape. When the sun peaked the horizon, she looked through the windshield, and realized she had stopped in an area that looked like a primitive parking lot. It was dusty and small. She had no idea what it was a parking lot for, and right then, she didn' t care. Running a hand through her short locks, she peered with groggy eyes at the landscape.

"What's wrong with me?" She spoke aloud; the absolute silence surrounding her made her aware of the isolation of this park. *Where am I? Out in the middle of nowhere,* Briana answered herself — silently this time. God only knew where she was.

Am I going insane?

Chapter Two

Sunrise was gorgeous, an awesome display of Mother Nature' s splendor, pale orange, mixed with deep coral and bright yellow. Briana ignored dawn's panorama and stared up at the pine-covered mountain stabbing the skyline in front of her car. It was stark, standing out dramatically against the pale blue sky and flatlands surrounding it.

She didn't know exactly where she was, but at least she was in a park…of sorts. Didn't look like one, but there was a beat-up sign off to the right that said "Skinwalkers Park". She'd never heard of it, wouldn't have expected to anyway since she wasn't from these parts, but it was really a strange name for a recreational area — even one located in no man' s land. *Must be Native American,* she mused. Her curiosity wasn't piqued enough to grab the map and look for it under the parks section. It was probably too small to be registered anyway.

There was absolutely nothing else but the mountain in sight, no benches or picnic tables, and no walking trails. *Well, I guess the path overgrown with shrub brush, leading straight towards the mountain, could be called a hiking trail.*

Not sure what to do, Briana was unexpectedly overcome by that restless urge. "Guess this time, I go for a walk." Speaking aloud didn't seem spooky now that daylight had arrived. She shrugged and shoved her stiff legs out of the car. Maybe a stroll would be refreshing, strange urgings or not.

A refreshing chill pervaded the air outside, a relief from the cramped quarters of the car. Her knees protested at first, but soon she was warmed up enough to enjoy the rustic surroundings. A rabbit hopped across the trail and Briana smiled to herself. This walk would be pleasant after all.

It was a good thirty minute hike to where the craggy mountain shot skyward at a steep angle. Thankfully, once she reached the base, she found steps carved into the mountain' s face; they angled up for several hundred feet, and then switched to a tiny, rocky pathway that wandered upward. She paused with one foot posed on the first step. *Now, why am I about to climb this mountain?* She couldn' t seem to find the answer within herself, yet something nudged at her mind, that singsong calling voice urged her onward.

Shaky at her own thoughts, Briana blanked her mind and started up the steep steps. Taking a breather, after at least an hour of trudging up the sharp incline, she glanced back down. Her car looked like a toy—she was getting pretty high up. *Why continue,* she asked herself, then shrugged? She didn't know why she wanted to attain the top, but she did. A momentary fuzzy memory of questioning her own actions made her pause, but she lost her mental grip on it just as quickly.

After many more minutes of strenuous walking, she stared upwards, surprised to see the opening of a large cave. She hadn't noticed that before, and she'd looked up more than once while climbing.

It took only a few more scrabbles up a steep incline to a wide ledge before she reached the cave's entrance. Didn't look like anything special, just a large gaping hole in the cliff face.

Then why did a ripple of alarm flash through her, like she was getting ready to enter a cave full of ferocious bears?

Shaking off her silly thoughts, Briana stepped inside with confidence. This was a public park; therefore, the cave had to be well-known, at least to the locals, and thus safe for tourists to investigate. An odd sensation struck her when she stepped inside, a wave of nausea and blurring of her vision. Was she dehydrated? She'd forgotten to bring the water bottle with her.

Thankfully, the interior was cool and felt good. The temperature outside had been rising quickly, and because of her rigorous hike, Briana had been feeling overheated and thirsty.

The huge rocky foyer closed in quickly after a few dozen feet, ending in a tunnel about arms-length wide. It made her edgy — this small entrance to who knew what. She hesitated, but something called to her and she went on as mindless as a male spider lusting after his large mate waiting upon her web. Briana walked briskly down the slightly inclining floor of the subterranean passage.

The lovely, smooth golden-brown rock wall drew her attention and she paused, running one hand down its cool surface, which was flawless as glass. She was stumped. How could Mother Nature create such seamless perfection? Could this place be an old mine? No, she answered herself, that didn't make sense; mines weren't works of art.

Another puzzle were the light fixtures attached to the stone walls every ten feet on either side. Their appearance was normal enough, translucent globes. But there were no electric cables, and Briana didn't see how lines could be buried beneath the rock face, or why anyone would go to that trouble and expense. Glancing into the small space between the globe and the rock wall, she saw a round bulb that looked like an opaque ball. It hung suspended, she could swear, in the center of the globe.

Withdrawing her face from the lighting fixture, she was truly puzzled. Maybe it was a new space-age apparatus that was supposed to look futuristic and magical, but in reality worked on a simple mechanism. If she did meet any park personnel, she was determined to find out the globe's secret.

Shrugging, she continued down the tunnel, which ended in a wide, open area; it looked like a large room, except its walls were composed of rock. Several tunnels extended out from it like the spokes of a wheel.

A figure stepped from the shadows at the far end and she jumped. Both his sudden appearance and the way he looked, startled her. He was handsome, with inky black hair that caressed his collarbones, and a physique any man would envy. He approached her slowly and she saw he was tall, at least half a head taller than her own five foot nine frame.

The faded jeans fit him just right, giving a hint of the muscular thighs beneath, while his royal blue polo shirt hugged his wide chest, outlining its sculpted contours. Were these clothes park staff would wear? She wasn' t sure, but asked, "Do you work here?" She waved a hand. "I didn't see a sign posted for entry time or any fees."

"You came."

He stared at her intensely. It seemed by his statement that he completely ignored her remarks. Although his presence was surprising and exciting, his words astonished her more than his appearance. Yet, she found herself still inventorying his body, temporarily ignoring his words as well. This close she could see his eyes, they were as lovely as his male physique. Golden-yellow eyes a girl could get lost in.

Shaking herself mentally, she said, "I don't know what you mean. You sound like you were expecting me."

"I was." He seemed puzzled. "You heard my call, that's why you came."

"Look, I really don't know what you're talking about. I've been on vacation all week, and I didn't receive any phone calls from a stranger before I left."

"Phone call?" His handsome brow knitted into wrinkles.

"Uh, what's your name?"

"Raynor."

"That's an unusual name."

"Yes, it means ' mighty army' ."

"I' m Briana."

"Briana," he repeated in a soft, sexy voice.

She tried to ignore the way his voice made her insides go mushy. "Well, Raynor, it seems as though you' ve got me mixed up with someone else." She snapped her fingers. "I've got it, you set up a meeting with a blind date here."

His brow smoothed, but his jaw clenched as if he were angry. "You are saying you do not recognize me?"

"Recognize…" Briana stopped herself and stared at him. By God, he did look familiar! But she couldn't figure out how, since she was also positive she'd never met the man until today. "I' m sorry, but I don' t know you."

"You deny the mating call, then?" Even his voice seemed laced with barely checked anger this time.

"Hey," she put out both hands and waved them. "I don't know what kind of game you're playing, but I think I've had just about enough." She turned to leave, but he moved before she could blink, blocking her way out.

"You will not leave until you tell me why you answered my call, then deny me now."

"Look, buster —"

"Raynor."

"Whatever. I've got a brown belt in Tae Kwon Do, so if you don't step out of the way, I' m going to bust your butt." *Even if it's awfully cute*, Briana couldn' t keep from thinking.

"You really don't know me." He seemed astonished.

She chuckled, she couldn't help it; the situation was so ludicrous. "You mean my threat cleared that up for you?"

He shook his head, causing that magnificent mane to fly about his shoulders in a sensual manner. "If you truly recognized me, you'd know I could tear your throat out in a microsecond."

Briana swallowed, her threatened throat clicking with dryness. "I think it's time for me to leave."

Suddenly he pounced, that was the only word that came to mind, and grabbed her nearer arm. His grip was tight, not hurtful, but she knew by examining the biceps connected to that strong hand, it'd take quite a fight to break loose.

Her gaze came up to lock with his golden orbs, and something in their depths told her he didn't lie. She shuddered. Deciding that reason might work, even with a madman, she asked softly, "You only want an explanation?"

He nodded, his restraint seemed barely in-check.

"I've never met you before today, right?"

"Just so."

She kept her voice low and pleasant. "Then, how can I know you?"

"You heard the call?"

The stress was too much. She was a woman alone, faced by this muscle-bound stranger, who insisted on asking her weird questions. Like he knew her! What did he want from her? His behavior was making her nervous. Her breath caught in her throat.

He tenderly wiped a lock of hair from her forehead. "You do not have to fear me, I will not harm you." His eyes went to the rock face behind her, his brow creased again in thought. "Perhaps you bumped you head and your memory has been affected."

She wanted to deny that, but maybe the safest course was to play along. "I did trip and bump my head earlier."

"Ah," he brushed her hair back at each temple. "There's no bruise." He smiled softly, "Which there wouldn't be, unless you fell very hard. It must have been a light bump."

Briana listened to his litany with a sense of familiarity and alarm. She'd always healed extremely fast, even bruises not hanging around long, unless she really hurt herself badly, as he stated. How would he know that? God, was he some kind of obsessive nut, who had followed her around back home and knew her life? Is that why he acted like he knew her? Had he dug into her past? Asked friends about her? The thought of some stranger barging into her world without her knowledge, made her queasy.

Taking a grip on her fear, she asked, "Since I am having problems with remembering, can you explain what this ' call' is?"

"Of course, my beloved." He released her arm and stepped back. He appeared to be trying to make her more comfortable with the situation, but she also knew he' d try to block her passage if she attempted to leave.

"The call is the feeling in your heart, when you know you are alone and no other but your mate can fill that void. It is the emotion of acute aloneness you perceive with every fiber of your being, even when you're having hot sex with someone else."

So far, he'd not said anything that an astute person couldn't surmise about a modern day, career woman. But then, his statements also hit home so solidly, she cringed inside. It was as if he'd crawled inside her head and read the secrets of her soul. Now, she was convinced he was some weirdo who had gotten obsessed with her.

"That's all very nebulous."

He smiled and gently tapped the side of her head, then drew a slow line to her left breast. "I am in your mind and your heart."

She didn't flinch from his touch, which she thought odd. It was as if they were old lovers and she was comfortable with his caress. "I don't understand."

His arm withdrew, but his sweet smile stayed. "I call to you in your dreams."

Briana's eyes popped open. Was that why she had this funny sense of recognition? *Don't be ridiculous*, she scolded herself. The man-thing in her dream had turned out to be a werewolf.

"You do remember something!"

His ecstatic look made her want to run, but she held her ground. She also wanted to understand.

She sighed. "I've been having these strange, irritating dreams ever since I was eighteen." His happy expression forced her next words out. "But, it wasn't you, just some dark stranger…until this morning."

"Ah. The dream changed?" At her nod, he asked, "How?"

"It was weird, really silly." She flushed pink, embarrassed to share even a smidgen of her erotic dream with a stranger. At his determined look, she threw her hands aimlessly into the air. "Okay, if you must know, it couldn' t have been you, because this man changed into a werewolf in my dream."

If she thought he looked happy before, she was mistaken; he practically glowed at her statement.

"You still don't recognize me?"

His hopeful tone set up a pang of guilt in her breast, which was really strange. Stamping it down with a dose of realism, she folded her arms, stared at him, and said, "So, now you' re trying to say you' re a werewolf?"

His worried expression came back. "Truly, you must have bumped your head hard."

"I've had enough of this." Her fright had fled with his utter nonsense; she was getting angry. "I' m leaving and if you try to stop me, you're going to have a fight on your hands."

"I will stop you by showing you what your heart already knows, but your head cannot remember." With that enigmatic statement, he tore the shirt from his chest, then quickly divested himself of his shoes and pants.

Briana was too shocked to make a move. He stripped naked in a few seconds, giving her no time to run. Besides, he was the most spectacular man she'd ever seen in the nude. Just examining his wide, muscular chest and other matching body parts stopped her cold. She refused to glance down at his...*male equipment*. She was sure that he was intent on rape and she did not need to encourage him.

Furtively, she glanced behind her. That was as good a direction as any to run. But Briana was aggravated at herself for not running when she had the best chance, as he stripped.

Raynor unexpectedly started trembling all over, which halted any further plans on her part. Her eyes came back to his body. She couldn't help it; he seemed to be in distress. But she still wasn't going near him.

His tremors turned into spasms that ripped through his whole body. Suddenly, he threw back his head and howled. *Yes, howled*, Briana dazedly realized. There were no other words to describe the wolf-like call. His form seemed to be surrounded by a haze, for she couldn' t see his body clearly any longer. Bright colors shot from the fog-like mass, beautiful, but somehow terrifying.

She couldn't have moved, even if she' d wanted to; she was too stunned and too damned curious. After a few more ticks of the clock, the mistiness cleared and she had a clear view of his body once more. Only, it wasn't the handsome, black-haired Raynor, it was *him* — the werewolf. His amber eyes shone within the cave's shadowy interior, looking far too intelligent for a legendary monster and eerily familiar.

Chapter Three

She should have turned and bolted before the fog cleared, or at least after she got a good look at the transformed Raynor. But she couldn't move an inch. He was magnificent, as physically attractive in his own way as his human counterpart. Thick black hair covered his massive body. He was a beautiful male animal, in the truest sense.

Briana's wandering eyes went *there*, to his male organ, which she'd avoided visual contact with earlier. While she stared, it rose slowly, pushing aside the hair hiding its large size. Her breath came in short pants and she swiped at her mouth. She was shocked when she glanced down at her hand. Spittle shone on the back of it. She was drooling!

She stumbled back a step. "What's happening to me?" she shouted, strangely unafraid of the beast facing her.

A thick, guttural, barely human voice came from the wolfman. "You are my mate. Come to me." It waved a furry hand at her.

Briana didn' t know if she were dreaming or going insane, but the fact that she did want to step into his embrace, that she wanted to wrap her legs around his hairy body and plunge herself down onto his hard cock shocked her to the core. This attraction terrified her, unlike his physical appearance, which she should be frightened of, but wasn' t. Real or not, she couldn't deal with this horror in any form.

Finally, Briana broke from her paralysis. Running swiftly past the beast, she entered another tunnel that shot into dark. Unknown territory. She didn't know why she didn' t run back the way she' d come in, but something pulled at her to continue in this new direction.

She ran for a full minute or so before she heard his voice calling to her. It sounded fully human; he must have metamorphosed back into the handsome Raynor.

Putting an extra spurt of energy into her run, Briana almost stumbled when she screeched to a halt upon entering another rocky room. This one was large, but strangely, several large comfortable looking couches lined one wall, and three heavily upholstered throne-like chairs faced the couches.

Turning, she quickly surveyed the room, surprised to see an arched opening, its foot wide facing carved with strange etchings. The elegant markings looked like writing. What lay beyond the arch was just as surprising. Trees and low growing bushes met her eyes. For a second, she was completely disoriented, then realized this must be some type of interior garden. Maybe, there'd be a place she could hide from the man/beast. His voice echoed; he seemed but mere feet away. Without hesitation Briana ran into the courtyard.

* * * * *

"Briana." He called her name over and over, to no avail. Raynor stepped into each of the tunnels which connected to the room. Her scent was in none of them. Pushing his head higher, he followed the scent of faint perfume to the edge of the portal.

He stared into a scene of ancient times. Heavy, jungle growth overran the area he could survey, and a six foot tall dinosaur ran by on strong, swift back legs. "No," he whispered aloud. "You cannot have gone there." She would not survive such a world, alone and unaware of her powers.

Turning quickly, he headed for the central passage, going through its tortuous path in record time.

The large inner sanctum was pleasant; its many pieces of heavily padded couches and chairs, plus several lush carpets underfoot, made it a welcome abode.

And a comfortable dwelling for the elders, who guarded the cave and the time portal.

"You are distressed, my son. Did your mate not come?" Bhaskar, the eldest and wisest of the three shapeshifters spoke. His tall, slender form was swathed in the guardians' ceremonial robe; his flowing white hair stark against the black material.

"Yes, but she ran into the portal."

"What?" Chao asked with alarm, his heavy Mediterranean accent evident even in that one spoken word.

"Explain," Gorna, the female elder encouraged kindly.

Raynor paced, his agitation too forceful to contain at a standstill. "She acted peculiar when she arrived. In fact," he eyed each in turn, "she acted like she didn't know what she was...nor did she have any idea who I was."

"This is very unusual."

"Stranger still," he looked Bhaskar in the eye. "She freaked out when I changed."

"Freaked out?" Gorna turned to Bhaskar, her waist length ice-blue locks fanning out around her as she moved.

"Was terrified," he answered. Turning to Raynor, Bhaskar said, "She doesn't get out much. I'm afraid the language of younger people confuses her."

Raynor bowed to Gorna. "I apologize."

"Father," he addressed Bhaskar in the fullest, respected title, one reserved for the wisest of elders. "Do you know why my mate would be so terrified of seeing my werewolf form?" He paused for a heartbeat. "I suspected she might have bumped her head, but I'm not sure."

"We must read her scent," Chao stated, getting up swiftly for one so old; the others followed just as spryly.

It didn't take long to gather in front of the portal, but it took much longer for the elders to sniff the air repeatedly and whisper in argumentative tones.

"We smell no injury, my son."

Raynor stared with surprise at the leader. "Then, what is wrong with her?"

"We sense an uninitiated." He paused, confusion in his red-brown eyes. "Also, she was never imprinted on us."

"What?" He stumbled over his words. "How can that be, Father?" He knew as well as the elders, shapeshifters came into their first shifting around the time of puberty. And imprinting—all shifters were brought to the elders for this ceremony within two years after their birth.

"Remember your first shifting, Raynor? It is not only a natural part of our being, the young must be guided by an experienced shifter."

"What are you saying?"

The three glanced at each other, then back to him. "Many years ago, there was a young couple who left their clan...they've never been heard from since. The elders' council picked up their essence through the years, but we've not sensed them in fifteen years."

"I did not know this was possible."

"Oh, very possible." Gorna chuckled. "But very unwise. To be alone without support of the clan members amongst so many humans..."

She did not need to finish her sentence. All shapeshifter children were brought up to believe in the unity of the clan. It was central to their survival.

"How—why would they do this?" he asked. *Why would any shapeshifters leave their clan and endanger themselves or any children to the humans?*

Bhaskar shrugged. "Who knows for sure? Perhaps they were rebels."

"Or maybe they didn't wish to be shifters," Raynor stated. He was horrified at such a thought. His parents had been enthusiastic teachers of their ways; it was hard to imagine shifters who did not wish to share their rich heritage with their children.

"Where did you hear this?" The leader's expression was concern exemplified.

"Rumors have a way of making the rounds." He shook his head. "All this time, Fathers, I thought it simply another myth about our people." His voice was hesitant when he asked, "You think she is the daughter of this couple?" If this were true, how sad for poor Briana. To never have known the love and caring of the clan, the history of the Reeshon, and to never experience the thrill of shifting—it was unfair that she missed all these wondrous practices and knowledge.

"Yes," Bhaskar nodded. "The entrance to the cave would not have opened, as well you know, if she were not a shifter. She would not even have seen it."

"Then how?" Raynor was truly puzzled over his mate, a shifter who was not truly a shifter, not yet at least.

Gorna picked up the thread of the conversation, "Her parents either died before teaching her to shift, or they chose not to teach her." Her sharp blue eyes became slightly sad. "Certainly, her parents never brought her for the imprinting."

He looked perturbed. "What would this do to her—not shifting as is her nature?"

Bhaskar's face was solemn. "She would be a restless spirit, never feeling as if she truly belonged anywhere. She would find no human male to her liking for long. And she would hear her mate's call as only a distant song, not a deep yearning she could not resist."

Raynor nodded in instant understanding. He'd often wondered over the past few years why it'd taken so long for his mate to respond. When he'd discerned her presence near at last, he'd come to the Cave of Immortality to await her arrival.

"I must go after her."

"Of course," the three acknowledged as one voice.

"How do I find the right time period?" Raynor couldn't keep the concern from his voice.

"We must meld our wills together, imprint her essence that still remains here, and when we have located her, we will tell you to go."

"How long will it take?" Raynor was worried. Briana could be, at this moment, getting attacked by some human from the past, or even more deadly, a savage beast from some ancient time. He must protect her at all costs. She was his. Briana was his chosen mate; no other would come along in his lifetime. And even though their mental contact had been sketchy at best through the years, he cared for her. Just meeting her briefly had cemented his feelings further—he wanted to make love to her, to fall in love with the bright, brave personality he'd caught only a glimpse of.

"Perhaps days, hours, even minutes." Bhaskar answered. The three smiled kindly, watching him pace.

"We don't have complete control over the portal, as you know, until a united couple is ready to leap through," Chao responded kindly. "But, by centering our powers on both of your essences, we can pinpoint a particular century and country. After that, we can locate the decade she's in. Then, we just wait until her being pierces the portal."

He ran one hand through his hair in frustration. "I remember my lessons. What do I…we do now?"

"We need to prepare you for your journey first." Gorna led him to a far corner where a large, gleaming mahogany cabinet stood. She opened it to expose many different items stashed inside, but withdrew only a few and handed them to him: a bag containing a collection of modern coins, another pack with food, and a water bottle.

The elder's hand flitted over the fabrics inside, and then pulled out a short-sleeved shirt. "I noticed you'd ripped yours." Her voice was edged with humor when she handed it to him. She added, "It wouldn't do for you to transport into a different time with torn clothes."

Raynor really didn't care, but he guessed trying to find needle and thread in a distant past could be a problem.

"Are these all I will need?" He changed his shirt quickly.

"Remember your lessons, my son. Only the basic necessities. You will need to secure any other items from the time period in which you find yourself."

He shook his head. That was true. No need to burden himself — he might have to come out fighting once he reached the other side. Also, the portal was limited by the amount of inert material it could send through. Jumpers had to carefully choose items to take with them, guided by the elders' vast knowledge.

The three elders strode quickly and took up positions in front of the portal, then joined hands. Raynor stood apart, knowing he should not interfere or break their concentration. He watched with genuine interest while ancestral time periods passed before their eyes. The portal switched into different eras every few minutes.

The question was, would the elders be able to locate Briana before she got into serious trouble?

Scene after scene flashed through the time portal's magical barrier: Civil War soldiers slaughtering each other across a sunflower-strewn field; Native Americans riding with flawless skill atop their painted ponies while they pursued a herd of buffalo; masses of dark-skinned people skillfully fitting a huge block into the side of a pyramid; a metal-clad knight riding swiftly past on a magnificent steed.

Bhaskar turned to catch his eye and said quietly, "She has passed into this century." He turned back and a glow emitted from their joined hands.

After a few more minutes, he remarked, "We have located the country."

A mere minute later, he said, "Now we know the decade."

The flickers of past lives went on for a good hour; the scenes centered on humans. By their clothes, he guessed the time period to be in the Medieval age. Many sights were so wondrous Raynor wished he would have time to explore them further, that he were not on a mission to save his beloved. Finally, the elders stirred, dropped their joined hands, and turned to him.

He knew without them saying a word, this was the timeframe, the point in time where Briana had jumped through the portal. Approaching the gateway quickly, before it had time to switch, he nodded respectfully to the elders, and then stepped through.

Chapter Four

Briana didn't know what to think once she stepped through that archway. The garden turned out to be something entirely different. No walls were visible, either cave-like or any kind of fencing or barrier that would normally bound such an area. The vista went on as far as she could see.

What was going on? She should have stepped into a courtyard. The cave couldn't open into land such as met her eyes. From the plant life, the place seemed to be of a temperate zone; the deeply rich, green color more indicative of England or Ireland than the United States. The area outside the cave was scrub brush and desert. Touching her head tentatively, she wondered if she'd truly bumped her head. Were knocked-unconscious dreams this bizarre? Taking a step, she paused in confusion again; she couldn't move, felt weighted down.

Glancing downward, Briana couldn't stop the squeak that escaped her lips. A long, flowing gown draped her form. She fumbled at her collarbone, feeling a weight there, and looking down, saw beautiful brooches on either side attached to it. Peering behind her, Briana realized the pins attached a gorgeous velvet cloak to the dress, its edges trimmed in what looked like fox fur. Something was on her head — she fingered some kind of cloth covering all her hair. What was going on? Had someone re-dressed her while she was apparently knocked out? She glanced quickly and fearfully around her; that crazy man wasn't in sight.

In fact—her eyes took in the whole circumference around her—not only was the wolfman not pursuing her any longer, no cave or mountain were in view either. A quiver ran down her spine. Neither was there the arch through which she'd passed.

Suddenly, fear ripped through her more powerfully than when Raynor had changed into a werewolf in front of her. Shivering, she pulled the cloak around her shoulders; it was quite chilly, which she found surprising since the greenery bespoke a summer season. Her cold body gave in to exhaustion.

Spying a large boulder nearby, she struggled with the heavy folds of material, finally gathering them in both hands and hiking them up high to make walking easier. Wearily, she sank onto the rock and hung her head for some moments. Thoughts of insanity crept back into her consciousness, but she quickly shook that off; she didn't really think she was crazy.

She just didn't know what to do. Nothing was recognizable, she had no idea where she was; she could be in Oz for all she knew. Briana had no idea how long she sat staring into space, but abruptly a loud popping, fizzling sound broke into her reverie. She started. She'd heard that noise before, when she walked through the archway.

A tickling sensation hit the back of her head, and she quickly turned the best she could with the cumbersome clothes and stared toward the crackling sound. A beautiful light display made up of slashes of icy blue lightning bolts shot from a grassy area between two great oak trees. Then *he* stepped from nowhere, into this place.

She must have had a premonition, for she was convinced it'd be him; she'd grabbed handfuls of the gown, ready to run when she saw for certain what had caused the strange noises. But once he appeared, she lost all thoughts of running and collapsed onto the boulder, deep laughter gripping her so hard her ribs hurt.

"What? Is it that bad?" Raynor glanced down at the apparel the time portal had "chosen" for him. His expression seemed to reflect it was indeed terrible. A loose-fitting tunic hit him at the knees and baggy hose rode his legs in crumpled disarray. These unsightly, uncomfortable things were worn on top of another pair of tight fitting hose. Fortunately, a decent pair of leather boots covered his lower legs, and a wide leather belt kept the voluminous material from flapping about him like a muumuu an old granny would wear.

He moaned in an exaggerated way and pulled at the tunic. "All modern items are changed once you step through the portal, including the coins, water flask and food. The clothes too, unfortunately."

The portal had done a poor job this time, it seemed. Looked like these clothes had been made for a much bigger man. Her giggles erupted and he eyed her sourly.

"This is your fault."

"My fault?" She wiped tears from the corners of her eyes.

"Yes, the portal picks up on the memories of the people who pass through, and 'chooses' those that are the most clear." He frowned and eyed her.

"What on Earth are you talking about?"

He walked closer. She became alert, watching him warily, but the smile that tugged her lips upward made it clear to him that she was not frightened of him, not yet.

He waved at his ill-fitting clothes and then at her lovely apparel. "One of us had buried memories of seeing clothes from this period. The time portal picked up on that and transposed our modern day clothes into these. If neither has a clear memory, then the portal chooses the appropriate clothing."

"I must be dreaming. It's the only thing that explains your ridiculous appearance. You look like a clown or maybe a jester." She shook her head, "That green-brown tunic just looks horrible with those muddy brown-colored hose." She caressed the silk of her gown. "I must say I like my own choice." She tugged at her head, "Although I'm not crazy about this hat."

"You're not dreaming." Raynor fingered the strange material clinging to his neck and head. "And, what is this?" He shoved it upward and off his head, then examined it. It was some kind of hooded clothing that fit snugly around his neck and ended in a wide piece that fit the upper chest. It did look like something a court jester would wear. He pitched it as far away as it would go, and then scratched the center of his chest furiously. "Damn, did this have to be made of wool?"

She giggled. "You shouldn't be itching," she noted, "if your clothes are true to the period, from what I recall, you should have a soft undershirt beneath the tunic."

"I do, but I'm allergic to wool."

"At least be glad for the cloak." She pointed to his back. "If you haven't noticed, it's cold here."

He peered over his shoulder, reached his hand around and pulled the woolen covering forward. "Great, more gay clothing."

"You're insulting our ancestors," she couldn't keep a giggle from escaping. Suddenly, she changed subjects, "So, Sherlock, if I' m not dreaming, then what?" She crinkled her brow, and then clenched her jaw in anger. "You must have given me some type of drug. I' m hallucinating."

He sighed. "No, you're not drugged either. This is all too real."

"Then where are we, and why these outfits?"

"The arch you went through was a time portal and we've been transported to a different time period. The magic embedded in the portal changes the clothes you wear and anything you carry with you, to match the historical era."

"You should be a novelist."

He smiled. "I know you still don't believe me, but believe this, whether this is real or a dream, we need to be moving on." He glanced skyward. "It'll be dark soon and we need to find shelter."

"Far be it for me to stop such a bizarre dream." She shrugged and struggled to her feet.

"Hard to get used to?" He glanced at her gown. At her nod, he added, "We could trade."

She eyed his clothing. "You do have freedom of movement, but no, I don't think so." She couldn't keep a smile from erupting. The very thought of him wearing this gown, that is if he could fit in it, was too much for her funny bone. She barely held in the laughter.

"My lady." He held out one arm in a courtly manner.

Playing along with the flavor of this dream, she laid one hand in the crook of his elbow, and threw a good portion of the dress over her other arm.

They walked for some time, and then came to a crude road, a dirt pathway with two ruts running down the center and animal tracks. He pointed to the markings. "Those are from small carts. The prints are cows, sheep, and horses."

"How do you know so much?"

"Worked on a farm one summer."

Their chitchat was interrupted by the appearance of two things. One was the ruins of a castle topping a high hill. Portions of it still stood in majestic splendor. Or so it appeared from this distance.

The second surprise was a small boy strolling towards them. He looked to be about ten years old, very scruffy and dirty; his clothes similar to Raynor's, but the tunic and hose were a duller brown color. "Good evening," he called cheerfully when they neared. Briana took to his charming smile immediately and she found his page boy hair endearing.

"Hello," they both answered. "Is there an inn nearby, my lad?" Raynor asked pleasantly.

"No," the boy shook his head. "My village is that way," he pointed back the way they'd come. "But, there are no lodgings. I'm sorry, my goodman, and my lady," he bowed elegantly for one so young.

"What about yon castle?"

The boy's brown eyes popped wide open. "No one lives there." He seemed to notice that Raynor examined the place with interest. "Don't go there, sir, it's cursed."

With that the boy took off at a quick sprint, as if just speaking of the place frightened him.

"Did you hear that?" She whispered to Raynor and tapped her head. "I heard myself, you, and even the boy speaking in middle English. I understood it in my head as modern day English, or American, but what came out of our mouths was real English."

"Real English?"

"I mean, like the people in England speak."

He shook his head in agreement. "The portal acts like a language transmitter, only it works inside our heads." At her confused look, he added, "Whatever language is spoken, the portal transposes it in our mind, so we *hear* the language we normally use. But what comes out of our mouth, is the language of the period." Staring at the castle in the distance he said, "That also means we're in good ol' England."

"My oh my, but this is turning into a doozy of a dream."

"Care to explore a cursed castle?"

"You couldn't keep me from it." She laughed, truly getting into the spirit of her extremely long dream. She felt animated with excitement. "What do you think we'll find—ghouls, goblins, or maybe some witches?"

He shrugged and she became quiet. No way was he going to inject realism again at this point. Would she really want to know the truth? Would she want to know that perhaps monsters did await their arrival, creatures just as real as both of them?

Most of the trail leading to the castle was rough and overgrown, like it hadn't been traversed in ages. Only a small swath through the center of the bushes had been cleared, indicating perhaps someone used it occasionally. *Good*, Raynor thought. He didn't need any meddling humans interfering with the time he spent with Briana. Plus, he didn't want to chance hurting even one human while here either. Even discounting the fact he wished no human harmed, there were the facts drilled into his head from his youth—that a shapeshifter who traveled to past eras, and then killed, could change human history.

While he had perfect control over his werewolf form within his own time period, there was less control when it came to the past. Besides, who knew what he might shift into? He didn' t; no one did until it happened. The only true way to control the animalistic, killing urges, the ones that hit shifters once they metamorphosed when they jumped through the portal, the only true control, once you slipped into the past, was by connecting with your mate. Merging the two essences helped tame the wild beast, so to speak. Of course there were harmless shapeshifters one could transform into, such as a fairy or elf.

His task was difficult, but necessary if they were to make it back through the portal. Only a mated couple that were in tune with one another could jump back through, and it had to be done together. To get "in tune" with Briana, he had to teach her control over her shifting. It would be a daunting task, since she wasn't even aware she was a shapeshifter.

To accomplish the melding of their spirits that must take place, they had to make love in human form. Raynor smiled to himself while they trudged ever upward. He'd always thought it ironic that his people had to shapeshift to the human form to truly bond. Maybe it was the influence of living on Earth for thousands of centuries, or the very spirit of Mother Earth who swayed them.

When they paused to stare up at the ruins of the ancient castle, he knew one thing: it'd be a very exciting journey to bonding. Shifters were highly sexual beings, and during the excitement phase, tended to shift into whatever form influenced them during that time period. Back home, he would always shift into a werewolf, but here, who knew? It would be an arduous, but mouth-watering labor, to train Briana to stay human when she burned with sexual desire.

Just thinking about his future task made him hard, and when his mate turned to point out features of the tall edifice, he was glad for the loosely-draped material of his tunic.

"It looks like it was savaged by war." Briana pointed at scarred holes riddling the structure.

He watched her surreptitiously while she talked with excitement about castles and how much she loved them when she was a child. How easy or hard would it be to get her just as excited about lovemaking? Would she be a lover who was slow to arouse, but super-hot once the fires of desire were lit? Or would she be easily turned on, a tigress in the sexual realm? Would she be a screamer, something he found especially arousing?

His eyes flicked over her figure, gratified anew by its promising curves. Her full breasts would more than fill his hands, and her womanly hips were made for gripping. He'd never cared for slim-hipped model types anyway. The full-figured 1950s woman was more to his liking and Briana fit that image to a tee.

Unconsciously, he licked his lower lip when he wondered if her nipples would be large pouting, dark nubs too large to take into his mouth, or tiny rosebuds, which could be sucked in with ease? Would the texture of those lovely tits be as full and promising as it looked, or would their weight pull them into drooping, less attractive shapes? Flitting downward, his eyes wandered over her waist and hips, as if by doing so, he could see beneath the material covering them.

He hoped her derriere would be cute and rounded, like it seemed to suggest. Next to gorgeous breasts, nothing turned him on as much as a lovely butt. His thoughts slid over her body, caressing her front side. Would her pussy be beautiful like her figure? Would it be trimmed neatly or would she wear it natural? A frisson of excitement shot through him while he idly thought about a shaved mons. Would she be so bold?

He expected her curls to be black since her hair was brown, but what lovely shade of pink would he discover once he spread her inner lips? A dark, sultry pink or a lighter, enticing color?

His cock throbbed against the clothing, rock-hard and pulsing. He ached to plunge it into Briana's softness, but now was definitely not the time. He had no idea exactly what she'd been saying to him the last few minutes, and didn't want to act as so many of his fellow males, coming up with a distracted "what". At a pause in her words, he said, "Briana, look at this," and then pointed to an arrow partially buried under rubble at their feet.

Her enthusiastic "oh" as she leaned down to retrieve it, gave him an opportunity to shut off his horny meanderings. That'd be all he'd need, change due to his heightened arousal before she was ready and jump her bones, probably scaring her to death in the process.

He stood peering down at the arrow with her, listening to her point out its ancient features, washing his being with appreciation of old war instruments and pushing out those of a sexual nature.

His eyes were drawn to the impressive castle, noting its details. Two round-shaped towers stood proudly, a connecting wall between them. As Briana had observed, parts of the walls were blackened and some stones were missing along the face of each structure. The tower on the left seemed to be in worse shape, so they headed for the other. They came across an old moat that thankfully had dried up, but a rank, mucky mess still sat in sludge-piles at the bottom.

Spying a drawbridge nearby, they approached its edge cautiously. It didn't look very safe—rotten boards were scattered along its length.

"I don't know." She chewed her bottom lip and peered into the moat, a frown of distaste on her lush mouth.

"Remember, this is a dream." He laughed. Better to keep the mood light and let her think it was only a dream for now. Perhaps when they got inside, the old tower would provide the secure shelter he sought; then he could properly explain matters to her. He added, "Besides, I think if we walk carefully where it looks intact, we'll be okay."

Chapter Five

She took his hand without further prompting, and though it was slow going, they made it across with no problem. He was itching to explore the old place, but dusk was falling quickly; they needed to find a secure lodging soon.

Passing through the gaping doorway was an exhilarating experience. There were no weapons along the walls, no furniture or artifacts, but still, the old entryway was fascinating in itself. The narrow steps on one side had crumbled — going up them to explore would be more dangerous than passing over the drawbridge. Raynor was running his hand along an old stone, examining its construction when Briana called him.

"Come look." She stood in a doorway covered with a heavy wool fabric. His hand ran along the makeshift door when they passed through. The fabric on the other side had been hung by several iron spikes being hammered into crevices between the stones overhead; crude, but effective.

"Strange," he muttered to himself. If he thought that was odd, he was shocked to find a large, partially furnished room on the other side of the curtain.

Several heavy-looking chairs, shaped like thrones, were scattered about the room. They looked austere and uncomfortable; fortunately, exquisitely embroidered pillows were placed on their hard seats. Two large tapestries with intricate designs — one a hunting scene, the other a knight on horseback—helped soften the back wall. A long, oak table made of planks, took up a good portion of the far wall. Four brass goblets were set upon its roughly-hewn surface and a large wooden bowl sat in the center, with small apples filling it.

A strange crunching sound drew his attention downward. The floor was dirt, but over the central area, a thick layer of straw had been laid. It was surprisingly sweet smelling; giving the room an outdoorsy feel. His mate examined the lighting system available and he drew near in curiosity. Several tall, thick candles were placed strategically around the room, held in place by a thin spike stuck into the wax center and attached to a metal pan. Additionally, two thin candles sat on the table, the bottom of each set inside a metal cup. *Crude, but quaint,* he thought wryly.

The only other lighting came from thin apertures in the walls, small windows he guessed. The sun had almost set, the feeble light filtering in helped very little. Soon, the room would be pitch black.

Raynor moved across the room and watched her. She was beautiful before, with her full-figure, but she was bewitching in the Medieval attire. She stopped in front of a small mirror, which couldn't have been over three feet by five feet in proportion and appeared to be gold gilt with a beveled edge. He only knew this because his grandmother had owned just such a mirror. The looking glass was propped up against a chair, so that most of the person' s body would be visible when they stood in front of it.

"That dark green makes your eyes look even more lovely." She blushed and he was happy to see she had a sense of modesty. Women who were unaware of their own attractiveness turned him on. And he liked women who blushed easily; it meant they had a streak of shyness running through them, something he found charming.

"No wonder I didn't like this...I think they called it a ' wimple' ." Briana fiddled with the odd-looking hat, finally taking it off and pitching it onto a chair.

"It is a gorgeous dress though." She smoothed one hand down the soft material.

Raynor would love to sleek his hand down her silk-draped skin, but now wasn't the time. He sighed. She turned this way and that, admiring the form-fitting dress beneath what appeared to be a fuller one over it. The underdress had tight-fitting wrist length sleeves, while the overdress had full sleeves reaching her elbows. Some kind of sexy-looking embroidered belt rode her hips and made her figure more apparent in spite of the full dress covering her. It was a weird-looking get up, but somehow he still found it exciting.

Thoughtfully, she touched the mirror. "The quality is poor compared to our modern day mirrors, but I believe this would be a very extravagant object for a medieval person to own."

"Guess I might as well get it over with."

"Huh?"

"Taking a gander at my costume."

She moved aside when he approached and he groaned aloud. It was a ridiculous outfit. Those hose, or leggings, whatever they were called, were the worst. No matter how much he tugged at them, they continually crept downward. Right now, they were doing a great imitation of his granny' s wrinkled knees.

"I've been thinking." She paused and squeezed in next to him so both were partly visible. "These remind me of costumes I saw at a Renaissance fair last year."

Slapping his head, he remarked, "That's why I look like a clown, you probably saw a jester or something."

She laughed. "No, I believe your tunic and hose are reminiscent of a merchant class medieval male, or perhaps a hunter. Think Robin Hood."

"Yikes, 'men in tights'."

She giggled.

"Why couldn't it have been a knight?" A wide grin stretched his mouth.

"Hmm. That would have been more interesting, but I'm sure you wouldn't be able to move about freely."

"You're right, all that metal…"

Suddenly, she shivered violently. "Are you all right?" Concern edged his voice.

She nodded, "Just cold."

"You're right, it has gotten chilly since the sun's almost down." He opened the pack of food he'd brought and stuck his hand in; it reappeared a few seconds later with a small wooden box. "I don't know what this is, but I couldn't find the butane lighter I stuck in here."

"You wouldn't, remember the transference thing with the portal?"

He chuckled, proud of her for remembering important facts he'd shared about the portal, even though she still acted as though it was all a crazy dream.

He lifted the lid of the box and dumped an odd assortment of items onto his palm.

"That looks like a fire-starting kit from the medieval period." At his look, she added, "I watched many recreations during the fair; one was the primitive way they started fire." She pointed to each object resting on his palm in succession. "That's a flint, piece of steel, tinder, and a scrap of cloth."

"Hmm. I think you know more about this period than you fessed up to."

"Well, I've read up on it before; it was a fascinating time."

"Fascinating, but frigging cold. Any idea how we're going to keep warm?" He rubbed his hands together.

"Over here." She waved him to a small area cleared of straw, situated between two of the massive chairs. "That's a brazier, if I remember correctly."

"A what?" Raynor stared at the odd looking object.

"A heater of sorts." She bent down and picked up a hammered metal bucket near the brazier and tilted it so he could look inside. "See, they used coal."

He was unconvinced, but said, "I guess we won't freeze our buns off." He glanced at the faint rays shooting through the tiny windows. "Better hurry or I won't be able to see what I'm doing." He squatted and cleared the ashes out of the strange contraption. Readying the tender afterwards, he wasn't sure what to do with the cloth, but with a shrug laid it on top of the tiny, dry sticks.

Unexpectedly, he asked, "Can you pinpoint our date?"

"No, but I think we're in the 14th century." She knelt down across from him and placed a hand on top of his to stop him. "Raynor, this place doesn't really look like a home, but it's been furnished for comfort."

He pointed toward one corner. "Did you get a look at that yet?"

Her breath caught in excitement. "What a wonderful bed." It was large, with bedposts and heavy drapery on each post. "Who would live in this ruined place?

"I don't think anyone does," he eyed her with humor. "I believe this is a lover's rendezvous."

"Oh." Her look changed from curious to worried. "What if they find us here? What if they don't like us being here? What if—"

He placed one finger gently over her lips. "Let's worry about that when the time comes." He nodded toward the curtained doorway, "We can't very well go back outside and search out a new place. It's getting cold in here, what do you think the night air is like?"

She sighed. "You're right. Maybe the people will be thoughtful. It was the age of chivalry."

He kept his eyes on the flint in his hand; he didn't put much faith in people's kindness to strangers, especially when sex or some other important activities were involved.

A shiver ripped through him and Raynor struck the flint hard against the steel, repeatedly, to no avail. A soft hand touched his.

"I think you're supposed to strike the steel at an angle, about a foot away, and you don't have to act like you're beating it up." She pushed his hands toward the tinder. "And closer, a little underneath it too, I think."

He gave her an inscrutable look and then repositioned himself. It took some effort, but finally a small spark jumped onto the tinder; he blew on it, but it went out anyway. After a few more such attempts, he was becoming very frustrated, and cold.

He struck the flint again. This time a few showering sparks flew onto the cloth and he blew gently. It burst into tiny flames.

"That's right, that' s how the man did it." She clapped her hands in glee.

"It would have helped if you remembered that earlier," he grumbled.

She shoved his shoulder. "Keep blowing gently before it goes out."

They watched in wonder when the small flame lit the tinder.

"Quick, put those small twigs onto it." He grabbed the small broken branches lying near the coal bucket and did just that, but couldn't stop himself from asking, "Do you want to do this?"

"Oh no, you're doing just fine."

After a few minutes, the blaze was strong enough that he added pieces of black coal. It was surprisingly effective, as long as they didn't stray too far away. They stood for a long time in front of the fire warming their bodies. "It's getting dark. Better light a few candles." Following that statement, he lit the end of a small branch and carefully walked with a cupped hand around the flame, to one of the tall candles. It lit greedily and Raynor put the flame to the other candle before the flame went out.

Afterwards, he squatted by the fire, warming his hands, then asked, "Aren't you hungry?"

She nodded cheerfully.

Ever the gentleman, he jumped up, but while he strode to the chair in which he'd plopped the food bag, his body started trembling.

"Quick, come back to the fire," she said with alarm. "You've caught a chill."

"No, it's not that." He turned to her with anxious eyes. He didn't want her to be terrified of him.

"I'm shifting."

She stumbled back a step, bumping into one of the hard chairs. "The werewolf!"

He moaned. Trying to hold back the metamorphosis was painful. Shaking his head, he said, "I don't know. It depends what is influencing me in this time period."

She grabbed one of the thick pillows and held it in front of her breast, in a protective gesture.

"Know this, Briana, I will not hurt you."

"How do you know?" Her statement was laced with anger and fright.

"Arrgh," he clutched his stomach. "I told you, a shifter would never harm his mate."

She stuck her fists into her waist. "Here you go again with that mate—" Briana cut herself off when he went into spasms. Abruptly a mist appeared around his form. Should she run? But where? It was true he hadn't hurt her before; besides, this was a dream, she reminded herself.

Waiting anxiously in spite of her self-reassurance, she stared intently to see what appeared once the fog lifted. Perhaps a nail-biting minute later, Raynor's muscular physique stood in front of her, unchanged as far as she could tell. She was so relieved. He was still dressed too; guess he didn't have time to strip.

Gazing down at his body, he lifted his hands to his face, running them all over it. His expression was as puzzled as she'd first felt but seconds ago. He glanced at her.

"I don't see any difference, Raynor, except...you're paler than you were."

"That's odd."

Her eyes opened in a startled reflex. "Say something."

"What?"

"Anything, just more than two words."

He looked at her with humor, then said, "You're the most beautiful, sexy woman I've ever had the pleasure of running into, and I'm so glad you're my—"

Holding up her hand to halt him, she let a trembling breath out. "You've got long, sharp teeth." She placed two of her fingers to her upper mouth. "Right there. That's what's different, that and the pale color."

Touching his mouth, he gave her an inscrutable look, and then strode quickly to the mirror. Grinning widely, Raynor nodded to himself. It was as he thought. He turned to her.

"I'm a vampire."

"What?! I thought you were a werewolf?"

He sighed. "Remember, I am influenced by the environment around me," he waved to the stoned room. "I guess this old castle did the trick."

She edged backwards a few steps. "Are vampires or werewolves more dangerous?"

"Neither, to you." He waved in her direction, "Come back to the fire, you're starting to tremble."

"I'm not cold, I feel sick. I think I'm scared to death."

He chuckled. "You're not going to die. Come warm up, my sweet."

Suddenly, she clutched her stomach with both arms. "I'm telling you I'm sick, like I'm going to throw up."

He became concerned and then alarmed when her trembles turned into violent spasms.

"Help me!" She reached one arm toward him with a panicked expression.

Raynor bounded across the room, gripped both her arms and tried to capture her gaze. He must explain, must guide her, for she was on the verge of her first shift. Probably it was the fear of being thrown into this chaotic world. She almost pitched from his hands so terrible were her spasms; her eyes were glazed and wild. There'd be no getting through to her in this state.

Quickly, he flipped her around and started unlacing her dress. Even in her fugue state she tried to fight his undressing, but this swiftly faded when the sharp pains of the first shifting struck her. It took a few minutes to struggle with the strange clothing and divest her of it.

The mist had enveloped her by the time he kicked the material aside; he'd get no clear view of her lovely form like he'd been dying to all along. He fumbled and found her hands within the fog, determined to hold on and give her what support he could. Regret hit him like a brick. No time to explain the process to her, or even tell her she was a shifter and what was about to happen to her. No time to reassure her that everything would be all right.

Briana's grip became stronger as she changed. It seemed she sensed his presence and was holding on with every fiber of her being. Only once did a scream emit from the protective veil, one that shot through him with an emotional agony. When the haze began to dissipate some minutes later, Raynor was shocked. He' d seen many shifters in his time, but never one as magnificent in his estimation, or as wild, as his mate standing before him.

Chapter Six

She stood a good two feet taller than him…at least with the way she balanced on her tail. For some reason, the old B movie "Lair of the White Worm" came to mind.

His beloved was a very enticing snakewoman.

Still the same fascinating face. Her sharp cheekbones, large eyes, and lush mouth gave her an extremely sexy look. The shiny brown hair was as it was before, creating a pixie sort of effect, on top of the sensual one—a strange, but very effective pairing. But those lovely, pale green eyes were different; the pupils slit-shaped and wicked.

The upper body…he was positive was the same. Looked like the same D-cup breasts, which jutted out proudly from her chest earlier, but the small dark pink nipples were hard nubs. And the same gently curving waist that flared into womanly hips. Only, those hips were now covered from the waist down with snake-patterned skin, an intriguing python-like composition. The dull red coloring matched well with her tanned skin and brown hair. The length of her snake body was nine to ten feet, the tail slimming down gradually, the end barely larger than his wrist.

"Do you like what you see?" While she spoke, her body swayed gently from side to side.

"Yes." Sexual desire laced his voice; he wanted her badly. Even noticing the long fangs when she spoke didn't deter his arousal. She could now match him fang for fang, he thought with humor. Those lips. God. Full and ruby red, as if she'd applied deep lipstick.

Her form slid closer, her head dipped and she rubbed it against his neck; then backed off. Lowering her body slightly, they were eye to eye. "You smell good. What are you?"

He smiled broadly and her reptilian eyes glued to his mouth.

Her tongue flicked out to touch her bottom lip and she answered for him, "A vampire, most exciting."

Raynor received the impression she'd "tasted" the air and picked up his vampire scent. "You're not afraid of me?"

A deep laugh rumbled from her. "I am not as the other."

"The other?"

"My other half. She is too frightened of life."

"And you're not."

"What about you, Raynor, my handsome vampire— are you afraid of fucking a snakewoman?" Her eyes flashed with laughter and desire.

It was surprising she knew what she was, but then something about this particular shifter seemed different from the beginning. She seemed older, smelled of ancient times, perhaps when gods and goddesses ruled the land. Her being was earthy and sensual. Certainly, he couldn't imagine Briana using the F-word in connection with the act of making love.

"I've wanted you in whatever form you appear, from the moment I set eyes on you."

"She wants you too, but her mind refuses to accept it." With that statement, she slithered closer, her body molded to his when she placed both hands on either side of his face. "Let me taste your shifter kissss," she hissed.

Something told him she'd made her words sibilant on purpose to arouse him further, which it did. When their lips met, a wildfire heat stirred between the soft tissues. Her tongue slid between them, prying his mouth wider. She tasted spicy and exotic. Not detecting her fangs, he moved his tongue around and realized hers retracted like a snake's; they were tucked neatly into the roof of her mouth.

His tongue kept rimming her mouth compulsively. Something was different. Amazingly, arousingly different. Slowly his brain found what his tongue had already discovered: she had no teeth in her mouth except the fangs! Then her tongue began a quivering dance in his mouth, driving even that wondrous thought from his mind. When it wound around first one fang, and then the other, lastly around his tongue, he thought he'd come right there without even undressing.

A hot hand slipped down his clothes and latched onto his cock. He throbbed against that inquisitive hand, moaned into her mouth, and tried to quiet his excitement so they could have a full session of sex.

Thrusting her from him slightly, he kissed his way down her neck, nipping with his fangs, but not piercing her flesh. Her skin was so soft, as smooth as the silk which had clad her body earlier. His hands circled her lovely breasts, squeezed gently, feeling their weight and firmness. Rubbing his hair against the areoles of each in succession, he could see her excitement; the nipples were hard and greedy for further exploration.

Complying happily, Raynor suckled on one, then another, if possible, his erection growing harder. Her long throat tilted backwards and she gripped his shoulders. Suddenly, she moaned and he matched her with one of his own.

Abruptly, she shoved him back gently and swooped down on his body with eager hands, helping him shed his clothes in record time. *Ah, why didn't I think of this earlier.* The texture of her skin against his was exquisite. Her upper body was silken, her lower slightly rough, tickling and erotic at the same time when her tail curled around him. She moved it about his body like a third hand, an extremely long hand capable of caressing one to two foot sections of his body all at one time.

She flowed down his body, positioning herself on what would have been knees if she were still human. Gazing up at him with a sultry face hot enough to start the tinder in the brazier, she stuck out her tongue and swirled it around one of his nipples. Raynor panted in a sexual excitement so strong his guts knotted.

He'd thought her tongue seemed long when they kissed, but he'd not seen it until now. She continued to lick at him, giving him time to appreciate her impressive appendage. It was thin and flexible; she'd easily be able to roll it into an "O". Her head was at his waistline, her tongue at his nipple—being a snakewoman definitely had its advantages, especially for the lucky male on the receiving end.

Slowly, her tongue worked its way down his abdomen; he clenched his stomach in anticipation. She withdrew her long appendage and nuzzled his cock for a few seconds, and then flicked it out again, taking his whole member into one of those rolls he'd thought about.

He groaned aloud. That flexible tongue was completely wrapped around him and she undulated it, while not moving an inch of her head.

She stared up at him the whole time, her green eyes wicked and knowing. She knew she was driving him crazy. Opening her mouth, she sucked her tongue back inside and him with it. It felt like tiny snakes were trying to eat him alive in her mouth, but oh man did it feel good, past good, unbelievable. No teeth to accidentally graze his sensitive flesh, only smooth gum and tongue.

Suddenly, he couldn't maintain his control any longer. He gripped her head on either side, shoved himself back and forth, inviting those snakes to partake of their dinner. The slick, wetness of her mouth sent shivers through him. A few rapid strokes and he was gone. His buttocks and neck tightened; Raynor climaxed in one explosive missile that filled her waiting mouth. He peered down at her now upturned face, an almost worshipful expression on his.

She let him plop out of her mouth, but kept her tongue around him, milking him gently, gathering the last of his cream onto her tongue and swallowing. Smiling like the Cheshire cat, she flipped that magnificent pink appendage back inside, then flicked a drop of moisture from her lush lower lip.

His knees were weak, he sank onto them, let his hands flop to her neckline.

"You taste as good as you smell."

"You're quite a woman." He gave her a quick, sweet kiss.

"Sssss-snakewoman." She pronounced it with a hiss and he knew she was teasing him.

"Snake goddess, if you wish." He chuckled. He placed one hand along her cheek and as she nuzzled it softly, gently, her sultry look turned loving. He turned her eyes up to his. "I' m sorry, I usually last at least half an hour."

Her head pitched backward in roiling laughter, and then those hypnotizing peridot-colored eyes came back to his. "I would be disappointed if you had." At his puzzled look, she continued, "It would mean you did not find my skills desirable enough."

Picking up one of her hands, he kissed the palm. "I could never find you undesirable. When you walk...or slither," he paused and he could see she knew he was teasing her now, "when you talk or sit, I desire you."

"I have not sat since appearing."

Raynor brought her palm back up and licked it. He did not wish to offend this wondrous creature. "It doesn't matter if it' s you or Briana, I desire both—equally." He hoped that settled it. He didn' t wish Briana to go through an inner conflict, a true one that only a shapeshifter could suffer, not like humans would experience.

Her full lips molded in a slight pout; then she said, "I am here; it is the snake goddess you desire now."

He couldn't keep the smile off his face. She' d used his own words, "snake goddess", and acknowledged with her statement that she' d be content if he desired her in her present form.

Pulling her into his arms, they spent a few minutes cuddling and discussing this world; Briana/snakewoman didn't much care for this plane—it was too cold for her. In fact, now that they'd cooled down from their intense session, she shivered and eyed the fire.

Before she could move out of his arms and stretch out in front of the brazier as she'd evinced a desire to, he stroked one breast, tweaking the nipple into a hard nub. Her eyes came up to his face, with curiosity and a hint of fire behind her orbs.

"Don't you want satisfaction as well, my goddess?"

"I thought you spent for the night."

When he shook his head no, he could see her excitement level rising. That tongue flowed down her chest, tickled his hand, and then slipped underneath to caress his palm. He guessed that was her way of returning the palm kiss he'd given her. He didn't stop kneading her breast, but almost halted when the end of her appendage wrapped around her own nipple and massaged it along with his fingers.

Suddenly, he was rock-hard and ready. Her eyes twinkled knowledgably, as if she guessed this. Maybe that was her intention with the breast lick.

He leaned down and their lips crashed in a hot, fluid kiss that was scorching in its intensity. Raynor lost track of time, only her hands and marvelous lips and tongue mattered. They could have been sitting in the middle of a fierce storm, and the cold bite of wind or icy rain on his body wouldn't have mattered. Heat. It was burning up in this freezing room.

Somehow, as if reading each other's thoughts, they got to their knees, continuing the onslaught of hands and lips. He wanted to kiss and lick her secret places as well, but not knowing exactly where a snakewoman's orifice was located, he didn't want to ruin the mood by asking.

She flowed up his body and positioned herself. It was too exciting, this not knowing; he chose not to look down to see what she was up to. Suddenly, something warm and wet slid onto his cock. Now he looked.

She'd slid her hidden slit onto him. Raynor moaned. It felt like a human woman's, the inside like wet silk, yet it was different. It seemed tighter and hotter. Maybe it was that snake part of her, or maybe it was simply being a shifter. Raynor had made love to many women in his life, but never a shifter. He'd run across a few, but wanted to save that special bonding for his mate.

Now, he was so damned glad he had waited.

Chapter Seven

Her tail came into play, rubbing his body along with her stroking fingers. Pushing backwards and holding his arms with her hands, she undulated, her stomach and hip area moving in a fluid motion that reminded him of a belly dancer.

Abruptly she halted all movement and stared at him with that wicked glint in her green eyes; he knew she was on the verge of doing something spectacular. And she did. Movement converged on his cock inside her. It seemed like a multitude of small, soft hands caressed him, making any movements from him or her unnecessary.

Raynor clenched his jaw in iron-hard control. Her every sexual move seemed designed to drive him over the edge. If not for the fact this was his second attempt, he wouldn't have been able to hold off a climax. It was the hardest thing he'd ever done, this effort to dampen his excitement. The old adage about baseball games came to mind, but it was almost impossible to wedge mental pictures of men in sports uniforms into his thoughts while her "snake hands" inside rippled up and down him. His balls were tight and he abruptly pulled her from him, making an abrupt sucking sound.

"What's the matter?" She pouted, her eyes slitting even further.

"If you want me to satisfy you this time, my goddess, you're going to have to lay off the inside massage for a bit."

She giggled and for a second, he saw a flash of Briana behind those lovely orbs.

He descended on her breasts, one at a time, licking each hardened nipple into tight nubs, and then repositioned her onto his cock. She slid on easily. Pushing her hips up and down, he orchestrated the movements fast and furious. When his hands came back up to grasp her breasts, she redirected the play, moving in slow, sensual rotations.

Suddenly, she pushed him backwards. His body landed hard, but she stayed with him, rode atop him, impaling herself on his engorged cock. From tip to base, he was besieged by gripping, slippery heat.

In this position, he had full access to her large breasts and he took advantage of it, kneading them softly, and then squeezing harder. She rammed herself up and down on him while her luscious boobs swung over his face. He loved her tits. Loved to draw on the nub, hear her groans erupt when he did. He pulled her down and sucked one small, pink nipple into his mouth. The gums around his fangs itched; he ached to shove them into her soft flesh, but resisted. It'd probably hurt like hell.

She groaned and inside those marvelous muscles of hers started moving again. He watched her face, knew she could no longer stave off her passion. Just knowing that she was near her peak threw his system into a fever matching her own. His hips plunged upward to meet her thrust, and then her "inner hands" gripped him so tight it hurt. The pain was momentary, a flash of intense sucking action against his sensitive cock that was well-worth the discomfort.

Her body pitched backwards, her hair tickling his legs and she screamed shrilly. He could distinguish no words, just a long, verbal eruption of pleasure. It was an unbelievably limber act and he gripped her waist tighter, shoving into her harder.

"My goddess!" Raynor released his load as he bellowed her nickname, satisfied that she had achieved her own orgasm. Each squirt of his juices was grasped by her insides, as if those "snake hands" milked the last of him, just as her artful tongue had done.

She collapsed onto his chest and he placed both arms about her in a soft hug. After a few minutes, he rolled them to the side so they still lay in each other's arms. She twirled his chest hair around her fingers and ran one finger around his hard nipple. She seemed fascinated with his male form. He watched her while he stroked her downy-skinned back.

"Were you satisfied?" he finally had to ask. He was quite sure she was, but then he wasn't familiar with snakewoman anatomy. Perhaps the intense orgasm she appeared to experience was normal for her kind. And then too, he seemed to always ask that silly question, no different than millions of his peers, who worried whether they satisfied their partner.

She gazed up at him, her eyes humorous and sleepy. "Yes, you are a wonderful lover."

"And, if you'll excuse the pun, you're hotter than an erupting volcano."

She smiled, sexy and sweet at the same time. She yawned, and then shivered.

"We'd better move closer to the fire," he eyed it over her shoulder. "Looks like it needs more coal anyway."

They jumped up quickly. Now that the hot sex was over, he was getting thoroughly chilled and was sure poor

Briana/snakewoman was even more so. Before they even reached the brazier, she began trembling violently and shifted in a few seconds. The shift back to human usually flowed much quicker than the change to whatever shifter form the shapeshifter metamorphosed into at the time, but Briana' s change was super-fast. He thought perhaps it was the cold; her human form would be less affected by the cold than her snake side.

His shift followed her the next minute, but his body still felt chilled to the bone. After he had thrown coals onto the fire, it warmed the space around them fairly quickly. Briana had grabbed the dress immediately after shifting, but held it in front of her body, facing him. She seemed too embarrassed to slip it on in front of him. He grinned. Didn' t she remember their fiery sex but moments ago?

By the confused look on her face, he thought perhaps she did, but didn't fully understand or acknowledge her role yet.

"Can you turn your back while I get dressed, please?"

"Sure," he pointed to the pile behind her. "But, you'll need to put on that slip thing first."

"The chemise. I forgot."

At the same time he turned toward the curtained doorway, his nerve endings shivered with alarm. There were shifters nearby.

The wool curtain was thrust sharply aside and four magnificent creatures entered in movements so swift they could only have been shapeshifters, even if their appearance hadn't made it obvious.

They were vampires, like him. Two males and two females. Fangs appeared when their lips drew back in a hissing warning, reminding him of spitting cats.

"Que faites-vouz ici?" The tall, blonde male spoke.

Raynor was startled when the man spoke French, but he certainly understood him well enough, even though he'd never taken a lesson in his life. The man had asked: "what are you doing here?" His thoughts flicked back to the vampire's question and he almost laughed. *Isn't it obvious to them what we were doing? But then I guess they wouldn't appreciate some other shifters having sex in their territory.* He glanced sideways quickly and then back to the group. Briana stood frozen in fear, the dress clutched to her chest.

Deciding to take the diplomatic approach, he said, "I'm sorry if we overstepped our bounds, but we recently jumped and sought shelter for the night." For a second, Raynor was rattled; he'd spoken proper French in response to the agitated man. But then he remembered the portal's astounding ability in the language department; he just didn't know why they were speaking French instead of English.

"Jumpers!" The short, redheaded woman physically spat on the ground.

Surprise flushed through him. Usually shifters were pleased to meet others of their kind who had traveled through time; many interesting stories were exchanged of their adventures.

The woman's disdain was odd.

"How dare you engage in sex within our domain?" The tall brown haired man stepped forward.

"We meant no disrespect." He stood his ground, and then shrugged. "We shifted shortly after entering, and you know how impossible it is to control oneself after that."

The tall blonde woman took a stance next to the brown-haired vampire, probably her mate. She pointed to Briana. "This one barely smells of shifter."

Raynor glanced at Briana. "This was her first shift."

"Liar!" the brown-haired vampire, who seemed to be the leader, said disdainfully. "That is impossible."

He sighed, didn't want to go into a detailed explanation of his and Briana's lives. Besides, he didn't care what they thought; it was none of their damned business.

The blonde said, "Maybe she is a gentle shifter; perhaps a fairy. I've heard their odor is light."

He stared back at them. Let them think what they wanted.

Edging forward, the redhead said with excitement, "I've always wanted to taste fairy blood, I've heard it is heavenly." She licked her lips, staring at Briana with a cold-blooded, hunter's look.

Recanting his earlier thoughts, Raynor realized these vamps did need to know the truth, that keeping their shifter identities secret might kill them. Disgust ripped through him even as he realized this. Shifters who killed those of their race were rare indeed. Such beasts were shunned and exiled from any contact with their fellow shapeshifters. Stuck as they were, they had little choice but to commune with the savage predators facing them.

"She is not fairy," he stated with a no nonsense tone. "But something older and more dangerous than all four of you put together." He hoped to back them off with the natural superstitious fear that shifters held towards the more ancient shapeshifters.

"Then why can't we smell it on her?" The leader stated angrily.

Sighing, he said impatiently, "I told you, it is her first shift. You can choose to believe it or not." If he were not fearful of Briana's fragility, he wouldn't be standing here arguing with them. He could probably fight two of them effectively if the vampires jumped them, but unless his mate shifted, they'd have no chance against four.

"I still say you're a liar," the brown-haired man said.

The shift came on with a gut-wrenching speed. He let it flow through him, his anger fueling a much swifter change than was usual for him. He saw immediately when he came out of metamorphosis, the group had gathered closer. He hissed as they'd done earlier, backing up the less dominant male and female a step.

A ripple in the air next to him alerted him to Briana's shift as well. He knew she was terrified and was heartily glad for that just now. He didn't need to glance aside and see when his mate attained her snakewoman shape; the vampires hissed as one and backed up several steps.

His side vision noted her hypnotic swaying movements, and then she sounded a huge sibilant release that put all their earlier efforts to shame.

The less dominant vampires took another step back. The two others looked fearful but held their ground.

Heaping fuel to the fire, he said, "She is not merely a snakewoman." He waved in her direction. "Can't you sense her power, she is a snake goddess?"

"One of the old gods," the redhead gasped in fear and ran to the curtain, her body poised at the entrance. The weaker male vampire stared between her and Briana, and then made a graceful stroll to take up position by his mate.

"Nonsense," the dominant female said vehemently, though her eyes denied her words.

Raynor shrugged. "Believe it or not," he echoed his earlier words. "But, do you want to see what it feels like to be swallowed whole by a 'snake woman'?" He emphasized the last two words for effect, clearly indicating he thought she was anything but a snake woman.

"Come on," the red haired vampire whispered fiercely to her companion, pulling on his shirt. "Let them have the place." With a hesitant glance at his friends, the male disappeared after his mate.

Raynor stared at the remaining pair, refusing to back down, but chose politeness instead of confrontation. "Perhaps you have another place in which we can spend the night?" He waved at the room. "We wouldn't wish to deprive you of your abode."

The vampires looked at each other, and then burst out laughing. "You think we live here." The leader sneered and threw back his cloak to expose the clothes underneath, the female following his example. "We are rich nobles in this century."

He saw the truth of his statement. The material covering their bodies consisted of silk and velvet, trimmed with fur. Rings bedecked their fingers and the lady wore an intricate cut metalwork necklace. Everything about them spoke wealth. He was confused.

"Then," again he waved at the room around them, "what is this place to you?"

The leader's face became angry; he didn't seem to like being questioned. But then he glanced at Briana's slithering form; she'd become agitated and moved back and forth behind Raynor's back.

Suddenly, the man grinned, a smile one would expect from some beast of the underworld. "We use it for pleasure."

"Oh," Raynor felt some relief. "I thought as much, a place for lovers to meet."

"Some of that, it's true," he replied. "But, more the pleasure of blood and death, than of sex."

"You bring humans here and kill them?" He couldn't keep the building anger from exploding.

He inhaled a deep breath; then almost hissed himself. They were killers. He could smell fresh human blood on their skin. He should have guessed it from their appearance and the evil expressions on their faces. But, even though he'd been told of such beasts in shifter classes, he' d not expected to run across any killers of humans; they were fairly rare. To have four such creatures facing him was disturbing in the extreme.

Chapter Eight

The couple chuckled, the woman speaking this time. "Not to this room. The torture chamber, as you would probably call it, is in the next tower. We keep this room for our own private council and pleasures." She eyed the bed in the corner, her lush lips drawn up in a sensual smile.

Suddenly, Raynor had a mental picture of all four caught up in a wild orgy. It sickened him. Not because orgies were forbidden to them, at least with humans, but once mated, the monogamous relationship between shifters was one of their most sacred traditions.

With mammoth control, he asked, "If you're wealthy, why not do your dirty business in your own castle?"

The woman shuddered in an exaggerated fashion. "Why, we'd never choose to live in a drafty old castle. This place is bad enough." Again, they smiled, Cheshire cats who'd stolen the cream. "Besides, its isolated location is perfect and its rumor of being cursed is ideal. Our manor house just would not do...the people are too superstitious and the servants always seem to gossip. You do see our problem?"

"The only problem I see is what we are going to work out." He looked around. "I don't like the idea of staying in your fun house, but like you said, its reputation will keep the natives away." He hated the thought of dealing with these vile, disgusting creatures. But nothing beat a cursed, haunted castle for keeping humans away.

They wore bored expressions now, as if they' d played the game long enough with him and were ready to move on.

"I' d like to stay here with my mate until we jump."

"Ridiculous!" the man exclaimed, his indignation returning quickly.

Raynor' s body became rigid with anger and he clenched his jaw. "Your attitude is pissing me off." His tone of voice was very firm. "You don' t live here, and we' re only going to be here a short time. We have no other secure place to go." He took a step forward. "If you don' t agree, then let' s straighten this out right now."

They looked at him nervously and then at each other, as if trying to make a decision.

His aggressive stance seemed to make an impression on them. He saw Briana out of the corner of his eye. She moved with whipcord speed, to within a dozen feet of the vampires, and snapped out her long tongue. A squeal emitted from the creature she' d entrapped with her appendage, and then she flipped it quickly into her mouth. A long, hairless tail flicked back and forth frantically between her lips. His mate seemed to make an exaggerated movement while she swallowed slowly, never taking her eyes from the couple.

He didn' t know if Briana did what she did out of her building agitation, out of an attempt to back them down with a display, or if she simply were hungry. But it worked. The woman screamed and the man blanched paler than his normal skin tone.

"William," she tugged at his sleeve frantically, "let them have whatever they want." She stared at Briana with terror stricken eyes. "You know I can' t stand rats." She shuddered, put one hand over her mouth, and ran out through the curtain.

"My wife has spoken." He smiled grimly. "Just make sure you stay out of our way. And I' d advise you to stay away from the tower next door." He paused and eyed them both. "And keep your mate under control." He nodded stiffly, and swiftly departed.

Snakewoman rubbed his back with her body and whispered fiercely, "I don' t like those vampires. They smell strange."

He turned to face her. "You are so right, my love."

"Hungry," she suddenly said, her tongue flicking her lower lip.

Raynor groaned inwardly. After two heavy sessions of sex, he was ready to relax. Add on the excitement and danger from the unexpected visitors, and he was ready to crash for the night.

His mate made a fast dart behind one of the chairs and came up with another rat. He said "thank you" silently; she wasn' t hungry for sex this time. Swallowing the large rodent took her only a few seconds. She' d definitely been putting on a dramatic show for the vamps earlier.

Queasiness gripped his stomach and he turned away. Watching her gleefully consume her nasty dinner took a strong constitution. He knelt down by the brazier and piled more coals onto, staring into the fire until he sensed her presence at his back. A crazy thought flitted through his mind — would his lovely snake goddess turn on him and devour him too? He knew very little of the old gods and goddesses, except they had great powers. Shrugging, he had to trust that she didn' t care for the taste of shifter, especially her sexual partner.

Snakewoman stretched out beside him, her face happy and content. She was well-fed and warm. He couldn' t help but glance at her lush lips—so glad she' d chosen to eat *after* they kissed. Turning to eye him, she took a deep breath.

"You are hungry." It was a fact, one he wasn' t truly aware of until she said it. His growling stomach was suddenly very noticeable to them both.

He shrugged. "I' ll eat after I shift."

"Poor Raynor." She stroked his arm. "It may be a long time before you change." She flowed upward to her snake knees and turned her elegant neck sideways. "Feed."

He wanted to deny her request, but her neck looked so inviting and her blood smelled like the sweetest ambrosia. His hands clutched the joining of her neck and shoulders; he paused for a few seconds, giving her time to change her mind. After a few heartbeats, one hand came up and pulled his head to her jugular.

With a groan, Raynor dove right in, there was no finesse in his vampire kiss; he sunk his teeth in with one strike. The warm liquid poured over his tongue, as sensual in its own way as the sexual act. He swallowed without thought, without guilt.

Minutes went by, filled with the rhythm of her magnificent heartbeat and the flow of her blood down his throat. Strangely, he was aware of her thoughts as well, as if he were listening in from a far distance. The words *need* and *desire* were intermingled with his name and memories of her tongue stroking his cock. She seemed to be as tuned into his feeding frenzy and the sexual sizzle it created as he.

Somehow, he sensed it was time to disconnect and he did so gently, licking the puncture marks afterward. She yawned and laid her head into his lap. He was ready to fall down in exhaustion too. Picking her large form up into his arms took some maneuvering, but she aided him by wrapping her tail around his waist.

He laid her on the soft mattress and then quickly covered her shivering body with several thick wool blankets, then a heavy fur throw that had been draped on the end of the bed. Next, he pulled the heavy brocade curtains, gathered at the posts, shut. Their body heat, plus the enclosed space, would help keep them warm. She snuggled down, facing him, watching with sleepy-eyed interest when he climbed in beside her. Bending down he softly kissed her neck and said, "Thank you."

She simply smiled, a sweet stretching of her sexy mouth that was quite surprising in her present form. Taking her into his arms, Raynor allowed sleep to pull him down immediately. No worried mind-wanderings would intrude tonight. His last thought was gratitude that his shifter abilities, even in a completely different form, could be controlled. Otherwise, he could have injured his mate, or at least drained her to a dangerous level.

"Vampires?"

He knew what she meant. "Don' t worry, my shifter abilities are finely-honed from years of use. I' ll hear them even in my sleep if they try to sneak up on us."

Without another comment, her eyelids closed and she curled into a ball.

* * * * *

Briana slept hard, but awoke the next morning recalling vague, disturbing dreams about snakes, werewolves, and vampires. It was a most unpleasant mixture of nightmarish images. She must have been exhausted to be as rested as she felt upon opening her eyes to daylight.

She was surprisingly toasty warm, except where her shoulder peeked from the covers. Readjusting the blanket, she bumped into something solid next to her. Turning her head slowly on the soft pillow, a shudder ripped through her upon spying the handsome Raynor fast asleep next to her. His very real presence brought reality crashing down on her. His amber eyes opened suddenly and he stared back at her.

"Good morning." He sounded cheerful, yet also cautious.

"Tell me this is all still a dream." Tears laced her quivering voice. She didn' t really believe that and didn' t think he' d confirm it either.

Sticking one arm from under the covers, he tenderly stroked her cheek with one finger. "It' s not a dream, and I think you know that now."

"What does this all mean...what am I?" A single, lonely tear ran down her cheek and he wiped it away gently.

Raising up, he propped himself on one elbow. "Are you ready for the truth?"

She nodded, too fragile-feeling to answer. If she didn' t keep a tight grip on herself, she was going to dissolve into a pitiful, crying bundle.

Pointing to his chest, then her blanketed one, he said, "I…you…are shifters."

Trying hard to keep further tears from gathering, she nodded for him to continue. *Am I a monster? Does that mean I'll turn into that horrible creature throughout my life?* Her eyes misted. How could she go on with her life if she never knew what to expect—like that creepy snakewoman appearing whenever she wanted. *What would my co-workers think?* That thought made her smile inside. Some of her fellow employees could stand to be scared to death. Shaking off her musings, she listened as Raynor answered her.

"We come from an alien race," he was saying, "called the Reeshon, one that crash landed here centuries ago. They were legendary scientists. Their specialty was studying time travel."

Her eyes circled the bed's interior space, comprehension sinking in about her surroundings. They had jumped through a time portal into another century. How wonderful—how frightening. Would they be able to jump back to the twenty-first century? Where they two hapless victims of some greater scheme? "Are we one of their experiments?"

"No." He shook his head. "Much of their technology was lost, but we did retain the time portal, which you and I passed through to get here."

"But why, why continue to study time if they were stuck here—that is right, isn't it?" She still couldn't accept she was a part of these alien beings. *How could I be?* She'd lived a normal, human life until she met Raynor. Only those weird dreams, which she now knew revolved around him, had been something different than her peers experienced. At least, none of her friends had ever shared such experiences with her. She desperately wanted to believe this was a bizarre dream, but it was too real to be. But how could she accept the reality Raynor offered?

"We continue because it was our ancestors' way — we record the information." He paused. "I guess if our people come looking for us one day, we'll have a great deal of good data to share."

"Why wouldn' t they know where your — "

He pointed to her and she corrected, "*Our* ancestors had landed?"

She wished she could shove his words back in his face. She wanted no part of this alien culture. She wanted to go back to her old life, no matter how stressful or boring. Being human was comfortable, and familiar.

He'd paused, waiting for her to accept his correction. His handsome face was serious, his eyes understanding, as if he knew her reluctance to accept her heritage. "Some of the knowledge of their flight has been lost from memory, but it appears their ship had mechanical problems and their navigational systems were shot."

"Hmmm, sounds familiar." The brow he shot upward and smile that tugged his molded lips, showed he appreciated her sardonic words.

"*Lost in Space*? Lots of sci fi movies?"

A smile threatened to spill from her in response to his silliness, but she felt too sad. Drawing her knees upward, she hugged her body, trying to comfort herself. Staring in thought, she asked, "Raynor, why do we shift? It's as if our bodies can' t decide what we want to be."

"This we don' t understand completely ourselves." He caressed her arm soothingly. "Our true selves, as our ancestors were, are tall, thin humanoids."

"Really? With large heads and black eyes?"

He peered at her and laughed. She realized her own eyes had grown larger when she widened them unconsciously.

He laughed. "No, just different. Our ancestors were able to metamorphose. Nobody knows why. Perhaps it started out as a protective mechanism, but then it probably made their scientific studies much easier."

"Huh?" Her thoughts were muddled. What exactly was he talking about? His expression was enthusiastic, while she was sure hers was nothing but confused.

"Think about it. They could travel to different planets and imitate the natives, so be inconspicuous."

"Am I understanding you correctly—that werewolves, vampires, and snakewomen—are imitations of alien species?" This was too much! What a bizarro world idea. Now he was laying claim to Earth's legends and myths?

Snapping his fingers, he said, "You got it. Where do you think human legends sprang from?"

"Us?" *Oh boy.* In a few sentences, he'd destroyed the joy of fairy tale stories. According to Raynor, most of the magical or beastly beings in these stories were based on the Reeshon—her ancestors. The magic of imaginary worlds just flew out the window, replaced with an even stranger realism.

"Exactly." He gave her a pleased smile. "There are times when a shifter will be seen by humans, no matter how careful we try to be."

"Like these medieval vampires try to hide their activities." Sadness and shame flashed through her. *How can I be a part of a race that produces such monsters?*

He grabbed both her arms and brought her eyes back to him. "No. They are not the norm in our society. Never think that." He gently caressed the hair by one temple, the actions of someone trying to sooth a frightened puppy. And she did feel as fragile as a small animal, not sure what its powerful master had in mind for it. What did being a Reeshon entail? What would it mean to her life? How would it change her?

Her eyes continued to hold his, seeking assurance.

"Do you want to hear more of our traditions?"

By his understanding look, he seemed to think she was on overload already. And she was.

She shook her head. "I feel so lost. I don' t know who or what I am. I' m not even human any longer." *What am I?* That thought kept flickering through her mind, like a song that got stuck, revolving round and round, until you want to scream "stop!"

"Part of you is," he said soothingly. "Whatever you shift into, you take a part of that essence into yourself." His hand stroked her arms, his eyes never left her face, his expression kind and caring.

Her eyes teared. "I want to feel human again, Raynor."

"How can I help?" He brushed a lock of hair from her cheek.

"I realize I barely know you…" She paused and dipped her eyes downward. "But the memory of that…other woman is so strong." Staring into space for a few seconds, she brought her eyes back to his face and captured his golden ones. "Make love to me, human to human."

Chapter Nine

His look was tender and a touch sad, as if he perceived her pain also. Leaning down, he placed feather soft kisses to her mouth, little nibbles that tickled and made heat swirl in her nipples. He was a wonderful kisser. Her insides felt mushy, as if heat concentrated there. Without thinking about morning breath, Briana opened her lips when his tongue nudged hers open. His mouth was sweet, tasting of exotic fruit. A shiver ran down her spine as his tongue stroked hers.

She pulled back and stared at him with wonder. "I hate to be crude, but how can your mouth taste so good in the morning?" She placed one hand in front of her mouth and breathed out. It too smelled like she'd just eaten fruit.

Smiling, he stroked her lower lip. "It is a wonderful byproduct of shifting. It seems to cleanse our system for at least a day afterwards."

Interested, she said, "If you could bottle this, you'd be a zillionaire."

"Hmmm." He stopped above her mouth and she saw that his interest did not lay in discussions of such matters. His tongue flicked her lower lip, slowly caressed it until a shiver of anticipation hit her stomach.

Briana opened her mouth to his invasive tongue, overpowered by its strong movements for a while. But, taking the initiative, she soon had him moaning when her tongue stroked and suckled his.

Moving down her body in slow motion, he licked and kissed his way to her breasts. His hands were gentle, rubbing in circular patterns that excited her nipples into hard nubs before his head descended on them. She'd never been treated so tenderly, as if she were a fragile flower, which would break under harsh treatment. It was as if he'd read her mind. She needed a gentle touch to wipe out the savage lovemaking of the snakewoman that ran rampant through her mind.

"Oh, yes, that feels so nice," she moaned.

He came back to her lips briefly and stared at her with his fiery amber eyes. His look made her clit twitch. "Do you wish something, my love?"

Arching her back and thrusting her breasts into his rigid chest, she said, "Only that you continue."

Raynor swirled his hands around each breast, squeezing gently. He pushed each upward in his grip, lapped on one nipple, and then quickly moved to the other, giving it licks. He repeated his actions several times, until each nipple received many flicks of his warm tongue. A deep ache stretched between her breasts, and ended in her clit, which throbbed unmercifully. Groaning slightly, she gazed at his black hair spilling around her breasts, then leaned her head back onto the pillow, rubbing it back and forth as pleasure built within her. A string was connected between her aching nipples and the throbbing rhythm of her lower body.

"God, I love your breasts," he muttered softly, staring up at her a second.

She looked at him. He continued to watch her face while he slurped one nub into his mouth. He sucked hard and then flicked her nipple rapidly.

"Oh." Her head flopped back down and her hips moved restlessly.

Seeming to sense her heightened arousal, Raynor withdrew from her breasts, the cold hitting her wet nipples. Strangely, it didn' t lessen the searing heat in them. Adjusting the covers over them, so the frigid air would be kept at bay, he positioned himself over her.

Briana was ready. She wanted to be fucked. Moving her hips upward without thinking, she said, "I want you."

With a skilled touch, he parted her and slowly penetrated her. She groaned; it felt so good, so right. His strokes were measured, at times miniscule, at others long and deep. Whichever way he moved, no matter the rhythm or strength, she ached for more, shoved her hips against him in greedy readiness.

Her pussy lips were swollen and she felt as if she wanted him all inside her. Not just his cock, but his whole body. It was an impossible thought, but she grabbed his butt and shoved him toward her, as if she really could fulfill such a desire. His hard flesh slid against her sensitive clit, torturing it deliciously and making it throb.

Suddenly, a dull pain in her stomach mixed with the immense pleasure; it was confusing for a few seconds. Once the grip of spasms hit her, Briana knew the snakewoman was about to take her place. "No!" Anger lit her voice, along with disappointment. *She* wanted Raynor. *She* wanted to experience all of him. *That* creature had already had the full measure of his wonderful lovemaking.

After she shifted, Briana stared from behind the snake eyes, seeing what she saw, sensing what the snakewoman did. It was not a strong feeling, but one as if she watched someone else from a distance. There was no help for it, she accepted her other self and settled down mentally to enjoy what she could of the sex act with the muscularly-built Raynor. One thing made her mood better. During the process of shifting, she saw glimpses of his face, watching her anxiously. Was that disappointment she' d seen on his face as well? She hoped so.

Through her strange eyes, she watched while her lover transformed, changing into a sexy vampire. His appearance turned the snakewoman on even more, and silently Briana had to admit he exuded an allure she reacted to as well. His stroking rhythm halted only during the change; his emerging vampire form took up the moves with just as much expertise. The interior walls of her unique sex grabbed his staff with vigor, making him groan aloud. The snakewoman worked the muscles like a masseur in a massage parlor, kneading, rubbing up and down, bunching those muscles so that his cock was pulled and pushed around in constant motion.

He panted. "Briana," he paused when she hissed upon hearing that name. "My snake goddess, if you insist on giving me such attention each time, I' ll never attain my famed thirty minute limit."

"Then don' t," she said with a wicked twist of her full lips. With that, she increased her tempo, making him groan even more. His organ increased in size slightly; he was close to climaxing.

What he didn' t know was that her actions of inner stimulation worked on her as well. She was not made as the other; her center of excitement was located in those very muscles she used on him.

She was slick around his cock, and the slapping, slurping noises made her grind her lower torso against him harder. She liked that sound. It made her want to bite, slash and tear at his muscular body in order to gain further sensation. But she restrained her primitive self, satisfied with pushing savagely onto his engorged cock, impaling herself deeper with each thrust. Her breathing was erratic pants. "Fuck me, hard," she screamed.

He plowed into her with fierce plunges and exploded inside her. Now she groaned, her head pitching backward when her slit convulsed around him.

They settled cozily into each other' s arms, and drifted off to sleep again.

* * * * *

When Briana opened her eyes, she was very warm; her eyes traveled upward, saw his arms encircling her. The remembrance of their lovemaking rushed into her conscious mind and she warmed even further; then a chill hit her when the snakewoman memory emerged too. Would she never be rid of that awful creature?

"Good morning."

His deep voice thrummed against her temple. It was a strange, yet reassuring sensation.

Raynor stuck one arm outside the cover. "It' s warmed up a bit, but I need to start the fire." She watched in admiration when he jumped swiftly to their clothes pile and redressed, shivering the whole time. It took him some minutes of fumbling to figure out the double layer of hose and the strange fastenings; he was cursing beneath his breath by the time he finished.

It took him much less time to restart the tinder than it had yesterday, but by the time the coals caught, he was shivering like someone with the flu. Bounding across the room, he plunged beneath the covers. Briana felt obligated to warm him up, placing her arms about him and rubbing his muscular biceps under the blankets.

After he stopped shivering, he said, "Thank you." He smiled and asked quietly, "Are you feeling better?"

Her eyes dipped in embarrassment, and then came bravely back up to meet his golden eyes. "Somewhat." Not wanting him to think she had mediocre feelings about their lovemaking, she added, "Thank you, too."

Thoughts flitted through her mind, some wondrous, some downright confusing. Their lovemaking was spectacular, the best she' d ever had, more powerful than she ever could have dreamed possible. But why did they have to be shapeshifters? Why these particular forms? Oh, if only they were both normal humans.

She asked, "Raynor, why did you change into a werewolf back home and a vampire in this time? Why did I shift into her?"

He settled her head onto his chest. "Each shifter appears to be born with a gene that is stronger in certain shapeshifting areas; mine was as a werewolf." He waved at the curtained bed. "In this era, I shift into whatever influences me the most. In this case a spooky castle evoked memories in my genes of vampires."

"Sounds very mystical."

"In many ways, mysticism is a function of the process—magic is part of our society. For example, the time portal runs on machinery hidden behind the walls and on solar power. But, the cave opening is invisible to humans, kept this way by a magic shield the elders conjure up."

"The elders?"

He laughed, the sound tickling her ear pleasantly. "Three very old shifters, who guard the cave and portal through their magic."

She sat up, propped on an elbow and looked at him, curiosity lancing through her. "How old?"

Blowing out a breath, he said, "I think they' re all close to a thousand."

"What!" *Unbelievable!* She purposely put sarcasm into her next words. "Then, that means I' ll live to be a Methuselah too?"

"No," he coughed, acting like he was trying to hide a laugh. "We live a long time, usually about two hundred years, but only shifters such as the elders live an extremely long time."

Her lips drew into a sneer. "Do I dare ask what kind of shifters they are?"

"No harm in knowing."

His smiling countenance made her sarcasm seem belittling, to him as well as to herself.

"Bhaskar is a dragon, Chao is a centaur, and Gorna is a unicorn."

Her mouth dropped open, and she collected herself. "What about the vampires — are they the same as what humans think they are?"

"You mean things like, do you have to stake them to kill them?" At her nod, he said, "No, shifters, in whatever form can be killed just like humans. But we are much stronger and faster, so it' s more difficult."

"No fear of crosses and staying out of the sunlight?"

"Nope. Those are all legends that sprang up." He grinned at her. "You noticed I had an image in the mirror?"

"Oh, yes, that' s right."

She stayed quiet a few minutes, listening to his calm breathing, wondering how she could go on in such a crazy world. What she once knew as reality, was no more; what she thought were myths and legends, were fact.

"And the snakewoman?"

"Her..." He paused. "I' m not sure, I' ve never run across her kind before." He stroked her arm softly. "She smells ancient, perhaps she is like the elders."

His voice had a reverent tone, which frightened her more than the fact she changed into that thing. Just what was this snakewoman? Suddenly, Briana didn' t want to delve further into that question. She switched tactics completely. "Aren' t you hungry?"

"What?" Raynor' s tone conveyed his momentary confusion, then he said, "Sure, let me run get the food pack."

He did run, bouncing back under the covers and then digging out fragrant bread. "There' s some kind of meat here, if you want it." He glanced up at her and dropped it back when she shook her head no.

Briana took a large hunk of the bread. It was delicious. He handed her the water flask to wash it down with.

Staring at the pack in his lap, he remarked, "We' re going to have to get more rations. We' re running low."

"But, you found me. Can' t we just jump back through the portal?"

His amber eyes captured hers. "I' m afraid not, there' s only one way we can go back. We must jump together, and be bonded as a couple."

"What are you talking about?" Her voice was shrill.

"The portal is kind of like a vast wheel—time cycles through it continuously. We have no power to pull up a certain time period like our ancestors did…that knowledge has been lost." Poor Briana. Would she ever fully understand her Reeshon heritage? Would she ever accept it without cringing or questioning?

"Sounds like more of your mumbo-jumbo to me. I went through just fine when I didn' t know what it was, and you came after me."

"Look, Briana…" He pointed at her, then at his chest. "In order for us to catch the elders' attention so they know which exact time frame we' re in, we have to be in tune with one another and mentally reach out to them." He sighed inwardly, just a tad frustrated with her stubborn stance. His earlier, kinder thought was gone, replaced by his own inability to make her understand or accept their roles.

"Okay, okay!" She threw her hands into the air. "What if I do accept this voo doo crap? How do we ' bond' ?"

He smiled. "We have to make love until we stay fully in human form—that is the sign that we are mentally bonded."

Her lips drew down into a sour expression. "You know, it sounds as if the males of your race concocted this whole thing."

Sighing, he said, "Think what you want, but do you want to really be stuck in the fourteenth century the rest of your life?" He was becoming more frustrated with her, but then a stab of guilt shot through him. He really couldn' t blame Briana. Latching onto the logical choice for blame, he silently cursed her parents for not teaching her about the Reeshon or her abilities as a shifter.

"No way!" She sat straight up, disregarding the fact that the covers slipped down, exposing her enticing breasts. She was clearly too agitated to care. "How long does this bonding process take?"

He frowned. "I don' t know...days, weeks." If she kept resisting the knowledge as she did, it could easily be months before they bonded. She would have to accept herself, him and their shapeshifter forms, in order to "tune in" with him, and he with her.

He' d try to explain again. "When we made love this morning, we both started out human, but we lost control."

"So, we have to practice, practice, practice, until we get it perfect?" Her tone was snide.

He nodded. He couldn' t stop the flash of uncertainty from showing on his face. He didn' t want to add to her agitation by letting her know there was so much more. There were many steps between where they were and fucking while staying in human form. Practice of a different sort. He just hoped Briana would have the patience to work with him.

Briana was pissed. None of this was her fault, but oh yes, she was the one who was going to have to pay. Screw a stranger until her brain exploded or something.

Thoroughly disgusted, she threw the covers back and ran to the brazier. Sorting through her clothes quickly, she yanked a piece up, fumbling as badly as Raynor had earlier with the strange trappings. Puzzlement washed her face. "Where's the underwear?" she snapped.

"Don't know, maybe the portal screwed up."

Glowering at him, she pounded a spot of dirt clinging to the dress. Briana wasn't too keen on running around with a bare bottom, especially in this cold, but she had no choice for now. Dressing quickly, she turned only when she was through, knowing she was blushing from head to toe. "Didn't you say we needed supplies?" She didn't even try to keep the coldness from her voice. Let him think what he wanted.

After he strolled over to warm up at the brazier, she turned her back. "Can you please lace this dress up?" Her words were polite, but her tone was snide. It was frustrating to think she would have to ask his help every time she got dressed. Picking up the headdress, she shook its wrinkles out. "Do I have to wear this? It's very uncomfortable." This time, her voice was laced with sheer frustration.

Completely ignoring her curt voice and sarcasm, he plucked a piece of his tunic. "Look what I'm wearing. Besides," he pointed to her head, "I don't believe women wore short hair in this period. Better keep it covered."

She sighed, attached the irritating thing to her head and stared into the coals. There were lots of things she didn't like so far about this century—no modern conveniences, no TV, no Starbucks to run in and grab a quick cup of fragrant coffee, no microwave to warm dinner up—her list could go on endlessly.

The fact she had to get help every time she dressed, just made her hate it more. She couldn't wait to get out of this primitive place. She sighed. If it meant screwing

Raynor at every turn, she guessed there could be worse ways to find her way back home again. With a wry smile to herself, Briana wished her solution was a simple click of her heels like Dorothy.

Chapter Ten

Raynor stuffed the flask into the pack, tied it at his waist, and then added the small bag containing coins. Walking briskly in front of her, he pushed the curtain aside cautiously and sniffed the air. Only then did he step through and wave her to follow.

"They' re not here?" she asked fearfully, not wishing to run into those nasty vamps again.

Sending his long black hair flying when he shook his head no, he moved cautiously across the adjoining hall to the other tower.

"Raynor, I' ve got to, you know..." She blushed when he looked back at her curiously. "Is there a bathroom?" she blurted out.

"Oh." He chuckled. "Guess that' d be a good idea before we explore further." He cocked one brow at her. "You do know they didn' t have bathrooms in castles, at least not the kind we' re used to?"

"I' m not a silly ninny. A bush will do." She was quickly discovering Raynor loved to tease her and though she usually didn' t mind teasing, right now she was about to wet herself.

Leading the way, he stepped through a tumbled wall of stones, coming out into an overgrown courtyard, then headed for a bush and paid not the least attention when she walked quickly to another far away. By the time she got her dress pulled up and crouched down, Briana was sure she was going to pee on herself, but she didn' t. Squatting and letting go was a vast relief. Trying to figure out how to dry off was not. Finally in frustration, she ripped a small piece from her chemise.

"You men have it much easier, just shake and dry," she grumbled after they met back at the tumbled opening.

He simply grinned, and then said, "Did I mention that shifting also means we have less bodily fluids and wastes to dispose of?"

"No, you didn' t." She peered back at the bush, which had served as her restroom. "But since our facilities here are so wonderful, I' m very glad to hear that."

He chuckled at her sarcasm.

Thrusting her hands out, she asked, "Can you pour some water over my hands, please?"

"I don' t know..." He plastered an overly concerned look on his fine face. "We don' t know when we' ll find fresh water."

"Oh get real. This is jolly old England, there' s got to be tons of water around." She wiggled her hands. "Besides, my hands are icky."

"All right, goddess." He pulled the flask from the bag and held it out.

She frowned at his use of that word, but at least he was complying with her wish. When he stopped, she shook her hands vigorously to dry them.

Raynor stood gazing in all directions and she turned in circles to see what he was staring at. It was the castle, or what was left of it. Three towers edged the courtyard, crumbled and blackened ruins. The largest was square-shaped, its gaping hole of a doorway looked like some gigantic monster crouching, ready to swallow them whole.

Briana knew her imagination was running overtime in this creepy atmosphere.

The other two round-shaped towers consisted of the one they'd slept in and the structure the vampires had warned them off. Now that she saw all three parts of what was left of the castle, she thought the two towers might be the old gate houses and the larger building, the main keep.

When she eyed her companion, he crooked one finger at her. "Aren't you dying to see what they have stashed next door?" Not waiting for her response, he disappeared through the gaping hole and headed for the other tower.

"Not particularly," she mumbled, suddenly picturing bodies stacked like cordwood. Darn his choice of words. But, she kept up anyway. There was something really spooky about this old castle.

He paused at a heavy wooden door which marked the entrance of the more ruined tower. She wished they had a door on theirs; it would make her feel safer. Pushing it open slowly, he stuck his head inside. She heard him take a deep breath. He reappeared and nodded. "No one home."

The door creaked when they went through, and Briana was so close to him, she bumped into his back when he stopped abruptly.

"Not much to see. We got a better deal."

She stepped around him and had to agree. Only one heavy gothic chair stood against the wall, and a twin of the table next door took up a large portion of the center area. Something tickled at her nose and she breathed in and wished she hadn't. Sneezing violently, she looked down at the smelly straw covered floor. It was filthy, unlike the fresh hay the other tower floor was strewn with.

"What gives?" Her brow creased in puzzlement. "Why the vast difference in furnishings and housekeeping?"

"I don' t know…" He paused, his look taking in all parts of the room. "Perhaps they spend more time in the other tower."

Kicking at the dirty straw, she remarked, "Or, maybe it' s just time for them to change the flooring." She thumped one finger against her jaw, trying to remember what she' d read in a textbook about what they used to cover the cold, damp floors. "I think they called these rushes."

Raynor strode to the table, his hand running over something lying on top. Curiously, she stepped carefully, picking her gown up high and stopped next to him. Rough pieces of rope lay strewn across each corner, their ends running under the edge. He leaned down and peered underneath.

"Looks like part of their fun house games," he said once he straightened, a frown of distaste on his fine lips.

"You mean…they tie people down on this table?" She gulped air, finding it hard to breathe properly. Just what kind of monsters were they? What did they really do with the poor humans they brought here?

He ran one finger along the nearest corner thoughtfully. "See this, looks like dried blood."

Briana tugged at his shirt, suddenly very scared and sick to her stomach. "Please, let' s get out of here."

"In a minute," he said absentmindedly, walking quickly to the chair.

Glancing at the brown stains made her lightheaded. Briana made a swift retreat to the door.

Tapping on the chair arm, he drew her attention. "More ropes." He picked up a strand of fiber and let it fall. There were ropes trailing across each arm. Squatting down, Raynor examined the chair' s legs.

"Ropes at the bottom," she said, her voice squeaking slightly.

He nodded, and then rejoined her at the entrance. "I knew there was a reason I didn' t like them."

At any other time, she would have appreciated his caustic remark. Her eyes flicked over the room one last time, searing it into her memory, just as Raynor appeared to be doing. The walls were mostly blackened ruins; in many areas, the stones had tumbled into piles, leaving gaping holes, admitting daylight. No candles were evident, so the vampires must do their dirty work during the day. Unlike fictional vampires, shifter vamps could easily go into the sunlight. Two braziers sat near the table, giving evidence that the creatures saw to their own comfort.

It no longer looked like an ancient room destroyed by time and war. It was the abode of evil. It smelled of death and decay, of decadent atrocities.

Shuddering, Briana exited quickly. Once she reached the end of the drawbridge, she practically ran down the steep hill, disregarding the danger. Raynor caught up with her at the bottom. He didn' t laugh or tease her as he might have normally done.

"Care to go to town?" He stuck out one arm in a courtly fashion.

Panting to catch her breath, Briana nodded and placed one hand through the crook of his arm. "Where are we going?"

"Thought we' d try the boy' s village."

She nodded. "Guess it' s as good a direction as the other. Who knows how far the next village might be?" Briana was happy he suggested they walk to the village. It would provide a welcome relief from the horror she' d barely glimpsed in that tower. And she wouldn' t mind a brisk walk, or seeing the sweet little boy they' d met again. She positioned the dress over her arm. "I sure hope it' s not too far." These wood-soled shoes were deadly to her sensitive feet. Maybe the villagers would have a shoe cobbler?

* * * * *

Birds serenaded them while they strolled along and multitudes of insects sang. They came across a variety of animals in their walk: a deer standing in the middle of the road, a rabbit munching grass by the path, and a pair of young squirrels who tumbled in wild play on the dusty track. Briana smiled more than once, letting the soothing sights of Mother Nature calm her agitation.

Their jaunt couldn' t have been over a mile before they saw signs of civilization. Rounding a bend in the road, they spotted houses off to the right: small cottages with A-shaped thatched roofs. "Do you think we' ll be welcomed?" she whispered, suddenly feeling very out-of-place in this medieval setting.

"You' re a lady and I' m a...a huntsman." His hesitation clearly indicated he didn' t really know what he was, and was again poking fun at his appearance. "Surely respectable folks in these parts."

When they entered the main thoroughfare through the village, she thought perhaps Raynor had been off a bit in his estimation. Several older people sat in front of their houses, working on various objects in their laps. Some were doing woodwork, others pottery, and one stitching a shirt. Each looked at them with surprise and suspicion when they passed by, and their "hellos" were exchanged with barely hospitable nods.

It appeared that only half the small cottages were occupied. The others looked neglected—straw needed replacing in large spots on the roofs, doors stood ajar, the interiors dark and empty of life. Briana shuddered when she realized that these had probably belonged to those taken by the Plague.

Unexpectedly, the boy who' d been so pleasant to them upon their arrival ran from a nearby field. "Hello," he called with enthusiasm. "What brings my lady and my goodman to our village?"

Raynor clapped him on the shoulder. "Need supplies, my boy." He rattled the coin bag, making the boy' s eyes light with interest.

Seeing his intense stare, she said, "Perhaps you can help us in exchange for a penny?" She hoped a penny was worth something in this time period as she supposed. He was such a cute little boy, and she realized he reminded her of a childhood playmate who moved away when she was nine. This boy had the same cheerful attitude and inquisitive nature.

His eyes became even rounder, confirming her suspicion of value. "Yes." He jumped up and down, ill containing his excitement.

She leaned down affectionately, her feelings more intense for his resemblance to Eddie. "I' d like to know the name of my benefactor?"

"Robert."

"What a nice name. I'm Briana and this is Raynor."

The boy executed a courtly bow. "Lady Briana and Goodman Raynor, I'm pleased to make your acquaintance."

Stifling a giggle, she said, "But I'm not a—"

Raynor interrupted her by placing one finger across her lips. She realized the wisdom of that action; Robert would never believe they were other than their clothes declared them. To state otherwise would have made him suspicious of their motives, and if not him, certainly the adults in the village.

"We're in need of food and a change of clothes, if that's possible."

Briana had been surreptitiously examining the older peasant's clothes and didn't see much hope there. Theirs were similar in make to Robert's. Not that she, or she was sure Raynor, would mind wearing them, but they had presented themselves as a lady and huntsman. The villagers' suspicions would run rampant if they tried to purchase peasant clothing.

"The food is no problem." He waved them to follow. "My father is a wonderful gardener and I'm sure he can spare some of our produce." He led them to a large field, filled with stunted, sparse-leafed peas.

"Are these full-grown?"

"Yes," the boy shook his head, pride shining in his eyes.

Raynor said, "But they don't look as big as the peas I'm familiar with."

Curiosity lit the boy's face. "Where do you hail from, sir? My father has the greenest thumb around these parts, that's why Lord William rewarded him with so much acreage for our own needs."

Raynor looked uncomfortable and Briana knew he felt silly he'd stuck his foot in his mouth, and insulted the boy's father in the process.

"My homeland is far, far away. I meant no disrespect to your father's abilities. Has there been a drought?"

"You really are from far away if you don't know about the cold weather affecting our land and how it withered many crops."

He shrugged. "We don' t have this problem where I' m from." He turned toward her. "We did wonder why it is so chilly here though it is summertime."

The boy shook his head, a wise look on his youthful features. "You are lucky, Sir, and I am lucky to have such a successful father."

"All this belongs to your father?"

The boy giggled. "No, to Lord William of Haworth."

"Is he about so high?" Raynor placed his hand at chest level, and added, "And does he have gray hair?"

Robert's hair flew like a corkscrew. "No, he is a man in his prime, tall as you, and hair like mine." The boy tugged at his own brown locks.

Briana had been eying Raynor during the exchange, wondering what he was up to. Now she knew. It sounded very likely that the vampire leader was this Lord William.

"Lad, does Lord William own the cursed castle as well?"

The boy nodded, his eyes gone large again. "You did not see any ghosts or evil spirits?" His voice trembled.

Chapter Eleven

"No, just wind rattling through the trees and odd creaks one hears in such old places." Raynor grinned at the young boy.

"You're much braver than I am," Robert said.

He smiled. "No need for you to be brave as a knight yet, as I'm sure you will be when you grow into a man." He fluffed the boy's hair. "Although, it's just the sort of place one might find buried treasure."

The boy glowed at his kind words, and then his eyes turned thoughtful at Raynor's mention of treasure. Turning, he ran like a rabbit into the center of the greenery and then came back a few minutes later, a tall, rough-looking man behind him.

The man was introduced as John. Briana liked him instantly, just like his son. He had the same kind eyes, and though coarse-looking in appearance, his manners were surprisingly refined for someone in his station. She watched how the boy helped with the exchange of information between the two men. Now she saw where Robert had learned his seemingly natural manners.

Briana observed Raynor's politeness and negotiating abilities as the exchange of coins for food took place. Strolling along beside Robert and his father, they selected vegetables from John's personal garden. He joked with the man and boy. In spite of the difference in culture and the centuries between them, lively conversation was no barrier. For some reason she began to think that he'd fit in well no matter where circumstances threw him. She pictured strolling with him into a fancy restaurant; her decked out in a cocktail dress, him in an Armani suit. And she was sure he'd get through the meal without making a fool of himself, too.

While the men continued their bartering, her meanderings stretched further. A beach scene came to mind. Raynor wearing a swimsuit—now that was worth considering. His muscularly-defined chest and brawny thighs would make him a mouth-watering treat. Then, her thoughts flitted back to their first meeting and how yummy he looked in those tight jeans. Unexpectedly, the prospect of gathering food didn't seem as interesting. Her clit beat erratically and she felt moist between the legs.

"Check this out," Raynor exclaimed, shoving an onion under her nose.

Her lovely daydreams were shattered and she sighed. "Yes, definitely an onion."

The variety was a nice surprise, especially after the boy's explanation of rough conditions for growing farm produce. They chose onions, cabbage, spinach, peas, and turnips. Also, she had to have a handful of the delicious looking beets, while Raynor went for the carrots.

The shocked look on his face was priceless when he pulled a carrot top up and small, purple carrots met his eyes, not the familiar orange ones. He pulled another bunch up and strange purplish carrots popped out again. Turning to John, he asked, "Are these the only carrots you have?"

"Yes," the man's brow furrowed. "I know of no other."

Raynor chuckled. "We have orange ones where we' re from."

"Really?" He looked surprised. "I would love to taste such strange carrots." Shrugging, he pointed toward a patch of lovely flowers. "Do you wish some violets and primrose as well?"

"Uh, not today."

Gathering their things, they waved goodbye. Raynor whispered to her, "Are they so desperate they eat flowers?"

"No, silly," she laughed. "Those are edible flowers."

"I prefer carrots, even weird purple ones."

They had passed John' s cottage and were at the end of his long barn, which attached to the back of his house, when Briana started trembling. Gripping her middle, she groaned.

"You' re not shifting here, are you?" Raynor shot a concerned glance around them.

"I' m suddenly ravenous."

"It' s the rats."

"What are you talking about?"

"Listen." He peered toward the barn, where rustlings were stirring the straw inside. "You' re hungry and your lunch is calling your shifter self."

"Great." Her trembling turned to spasms and her eyes widened in fear. "What' ll we do?"

Pulling open the small barn door, he undid her gown quickly and shoved her quickly inside. "Do your thing and I' ll watch the door."

"Gee, tha—" Her words were cut off abruptly as she clutched her middle.

* * * * *

Fortunately, the barn was at the edge of the village, and not one person wandered by while he waited. Loud rustling sounds erupted every few seconds from inside, and his gut churned when he pictured the havoc the snakewoman was wrecking on the rat population.

After ten minutes or so, Briana reappeared, her cheeks flushed with embarrassment. "We can leave now." She side-stepped surreptitiously to his front so he could lace her up.

He chose not to make a cute quip or tease her, she felt bad enough.

The gown was smudged with new dirty spots, which she noted immediately, making a face while she dusted at each with little success. "Hey." She punched his shoulder lightly. "We forgot to ask about clothing."

"No I didn' t. I asked John while we were commiserating over the peas and you were talking to Robert over the beets."

"Oh." She raised a brow. "So, what' d you find out?"

"Some of the ladies make clothes, but only peasant wear." He eyed her silk trappings. "I' m not sure you' d like them.

"You must think I' m a snob."

"No." He scratched at his chest. "I just don' t think you' d appreciate wool like I do." Of course he didn' t think she was a snob, but it provided too good of an opportunity to tease her. He liked to hear her laugh. Poor Briana had been slapped with too many hard, new realities in the last two days.

She had to giggle.

"But, we can walk to a nearby town. They have shops where we can order clothes made."

"How long will that take? This dress is beginning to look pretty grungy."

Shrugging, he said, "Don' t know, but I can go tomorrow."

"What about me?"

"You can go if you wish, but it' s a five mile hike." He glanced down at her delicately made shoes. "And I remember you complaining on the way here how uncomfortable those are for walking." He ogled her. "Of course, I could carry you." He really must remember to look for a new pair of shoes for her. Briana' s clothing was lovely, but she' d had trouble getting used to it, and the shoes were hopelessly ineffectual when it came to walking but a short distance.

Laughing, she said, "I don' t think so." Then sighing, she said, "This ' helpless female' stuff gets old."

"Tell me about it." He laughed. He knew she wouldn' t whine about circumstances; she wasn' t a complainer. Another reason he was beginning to like her so much. Even though Briana had a hard time accepting her shapeshifter self, she' d taken the bull by the horn, when it came to facing the problems this century threw at them. She didn' t say "poor me", but turned the problems into a joke. But then she was willing to work with him in trying to come up with solutions to those problems. Such a woman was worth having at one' s side, whether it be in jumps, or in marriage.

Smiling along with him, she punched his shoulder again, a bit harder this time.

"Ouch." He grabbed his shoulder in an exaggerated fashion.

* * * * *

True to his word, Raynor left early the next day, while she sat contemplating the small scratched pot he' d managed to secure in the village. Running a hand inside, it came back clear. At least it looked clean, which was good since she had no idea where to get water to scrub it if she wanted. Even stranger, it was some type of pottery. The woman they' d purchased it from assured them it was a cooking pot, giving them disbelieving looks when they asked. She didn' t understand how it would withstand heat, but she' d give it a go over the fire.

Taking the crude knife he' d also bought, she began scraping various vegetables. What she wouldn' t do for a real peeler! Too many flakes of vegetable matter were deposited at her feet by the time she finished. Cutting the vegetable into chunks, she added most of the water from the flask. They' d refilled it from the well in the center of the village before leaving, and an old man had sold them another made of leather, which Raynor carried with him now.

For a long time, she sat in one of the gothic chairs, puffy pillow stuffed behind her back and thought about her lover. Her life had been turned topsy-turvy in just one day. Thank goodness, she had such a strong male at her side. Those vampires were frightening, and so was the snakewoman. But, Raynor had stood his ground, even against greater odds.

Although her lovemaking memories as seen and felt through the snakewoman were vague, she went over the details she could recall. How hard and muscular his chest had felt beneath her caresses. How steely his large cock was, and the power behind his thrusts. Of course, she had experienced their sexual encounter initially as a human this morning, but the snakewoman had more time with him, and she was jealous of those moments. She wanted to grasp their heat for her own. With yearning she remembered the burning desire their twined lips evoked. Squirming in the chair, she became aware of her throbbing lips, the clit beating an erotic rhythm between her soft folds.

Glancing toward the curtained door, she became uncomfortable with the thought of being caught in a tranquil sexual haze. Would the vampires return in spite of their forced invite? The dreariness of the cold fortress seeped into her body, made her think of things that slunk in dark corners. Just like that, her turned on state melted in the face of her fear. When would Raynor return?

Going outside, but avoiding the other tower, she found a profusion of lovely wildflowers. Dumping the apples from the bowl on the table, she arranged the colorful buds; it made the area more cheerful and elevated her mood too. She arranged the apples in a line along the edge of the table; perhaps seeing them would remind her and Raynor the fruit needed to be eaten before it went bad.

She frittered away the rest of the evening dusting the bed linens, and keeping a close eye over the vegetables simmering over the brazier.

"Honey, I' m home."

His voice was most welcome and she ran to the door to greet him.

"Thank God you' re back."

He gave her a lopsided grin. Raynor made her feel safe; this place was spooky. And he made her feel wanted, which she really needed right now. To be seen, heard, and felt as a human woman. He' d always managed to do that, even in the short time they' d been together. He listened to her and told her he loved the way she looked. And he was in tune with her feelings, making soothing remarks when he thought they were called for, or teasing her to lighten her mood. Under normal circumstances, she wouldn' t have stood for such coddling, especially from someone she barely knew, but this experience called for a whole new way of acceptance. Then, there were those vamps. Only when Raynor was around did she feel unafraid. His large frame was very reassuring.

A bundle was tied to his waist and Briana was too anxious to see what he' d brought back. Did he manage to find her a new dress? Shoes? Excitement over his purchases would help shake loose the last of the willies that had hit her earlier.

Pulling material from the bundle, he handed it to her while he dug further. Her questioning look gave him pause and he said, "A change of clothing for me."

"Where' s mine?"

"Oh, look, some soap." He handed her a rough-looking block.

She sniffed it. "It smells like...oil, are you sure it' s soap?"

"Positive. The shopkeeper said it' s imported and made of olive oil. Very expensive stuff." He fumbled in the bottom of the bundle. "Look, priceless items."

Frowning, she fingered the big hook laying in his hand, a metal ball and some twine. "Why is all that priceless?"

"Because…" He had an excited look in his eyes. "I' ll be able to put some meat on the table." He held up the hook. "This is a fishing hook."

"I can see that." His enthusiasm mirrored Robert' s earlier, boyish and cute. At least he didn' t intend for her to starve. She smiled at that. Caveman bring home meat to woman.

"This is the fishing line and this is the sinker." He poked at the articles. "I wish I could take these back with me. The line is made from nettles and hemp. I don' t even know what nettles are, but it was really fascinating listening to the old man explain how it' s made — after I asked of course." He glanced up at her. "Do you want to hear how they make the line?"

"Not particularly. What I want to see is a new dress." The dress she wore was really feeling grungy; she couldn' t wait to change into something else. And, she wanted to see if Raynor' s selection of clothes matched up to her earlier assumptions about him. If he chose well, he had taste; if not, perhaps she' d have to downgrade her judgment of his ability to make it through a fancy restaurant without spaghetti sauce dribbling down his tie.

He shrugged nonchalantly. "Oh, the lady will have it made in a few days."

"A few days!" She jabbed a finger into his chest. "How did *you* manage to come back with a change of clothes?"

Chuckling, he held up his hands as if in self-defense. "Hey, they don' t have clothes sitting on shelves in this time, you have to special order them." He plucked at his tunic. "I was darn lucky. This fellow ordered a new set of clothing, but then he died a few days ago of the Plague."

"The Black Plague!" She couldn' t keep the squeal from her voice. My God, was he really talking so casually about that deadly disease that wiped out half of Europe? She glanced around at the dust coating the furniture, as if seeing it for the first time. Could the germs be all around them? "Jeez Louise, we need to get out of this place."

"Uh huh." Finally, he seemed to take notice of her panic. "Nothing to worry about, shifters don' t catch human diseases."

"None, not even the Plague?"

He shook his head, his face serious.

"Wait." She thrust both hands in front of her in halting signal. "She...I ate rats...what if one of them had the Plague?" How could she not catch the Plague when the snakewoman had consumed God only knew how many of those filthy, disease carrying rodents?

"Technically, it' d be a flea carried on the rat, but it still wouldn' t infect you."

Trying to calm herself, she wished to goodness he' d just told her that right off the bat. Sometimes he had a way of drawing a subject out that caused her thoughts to go flying off in crazy directions, and worrying her for nothing.

She stared at his clothes anew. "Well, aren' t you the lucky one?" Her sarcasm pulled another chuckle from him. Picking up the wimple, which she hated, she flapped it in the air, as if trying to shake the wrinkles out. She could care less, but she couldn' t shake her dress to make her point. Damn, he was hard-headed sometimes. Or oblivious. Or just a man.

"Yeah, I was, but that poor guy wasn' t," he said over her flapping.

"Quit trying to change the subject." She held out the skirt of the dress. "What am I supposed to do? This thing is filthy."

"Voila." He plucked the soap from the chair where she' d thrown it. "Laundry day tomorrow."

Crossing her arms, she stared at him. "And just where are we supposed to get enough water to accomplish that?"

Examining the items in his palm, Raynor didn' t even look up when he answered, "There' s a stream about half a mile behind the ruins."

"My, my, you' re a fount of information. I' ll have to go with you next time." *That' s the only way I' ll really find out all the information I need.*

"Yes, you' d love it, very quaint."

"You' re loving this historical jump, aren' t you?"

"As a matter of fact, I am." He gave her a curious look. "I thought you were too."

Throwing her hands into the air, she exclaimed, "I was until I kept getting held back by all these feminine encumbrances!" Well, she acceded to herself, it wasn' t *that* bad, just aggravating. A pair of jeans, tee shirt, and gym shoes were so much better for comfort and things like walking long distances.

He glanced downward, "Speaking of that, you can' t go back with me the next trip, you forgot about your shoes."

Placing her hands at her waist, she huffed, "If *someone* had thought to buy me a comfortable pair, I could."

"I did the best I could." He looked at her with a funny expression on his handsome face. "I ran out of money."

"Oh, is that right?" Her face flushed with anger. "But you managed to buy your clothes and your fishing equipment first."

Sighing, he put the items on the chair and took her arms into his large hands. "Look, I'm sorry I couldn't bring a dress back, it was just too expensive. I had to leave the money I had left as a deposit." He stroked her arms gently, "And I'm sorry things have been so difficult for you here."

Her features calmed, but then she frowned. "How are we going to pay for the dress, then?"

He looked at her, an inscrutable glint in his eyes. "I've been thinking about that...I don't guess there's any need for a gym manager."

"And I'm a hotel manager," Briana stated.

Nodding, he said, "Even if we could find a hotel, or rather an inn management position, they wouldn't hire a lady."

"Thanks for reminding me of my *position* here."

Raynor smiled at her humorous sarcasm. "I..." He paused and gave her a strange look. "I thought maybe we could be exterminators."

Chapter Twelve

"What? Exterminators!" She laughed. "Raynor, in case you haven' t noticed, these people aren' t the cleanest in the world. I hardly think a few fleas and rats would bother them." She halted when his eyes twinkled merrily. "Oh, no, you can' t be thinking what I think you' re thinking."

He waved one hand at her. "You' re a natural."

"Thanks," she said sarcastically. God help her, he was serious.

"At least the snakewoman is. She knows where to find vermin and she' s the best exterminator I' ve ever seen."

"You take the cake!"

"Well, what else are we going to do to earn money?"

Briana' s mind wheeled. Guess they could see if John needed any help with the gardens, but then she knew nothing about raising vegetables. She caught his eye. "Do you know anything about gardening?"

At his negative shake of his head, she mumbled, "Thought not." She couldn' t sew, so seamstress was out. A prostitute? No way. *Can you imagine the stench of the men?* She sighed inwardly. Even if the men were handsome with perfect bathing habits, she still wouldn' t be able to fuck a total stranger. She glanced at Raynor. He was different, even though he was barely past a stranger to her. He was a shapeshifter, as she was, a fact she was beginning to accept. And according to him, his mate. She didn' t disagree with that statement as she had the first time they met. She felt too drawn to him. He set her blood on fire as no other man had before. And darn it, she liked him, very much.

Interjecting into her stewing mind, he said, "You know, you have a really lovely new dress waiting for me to pick up in three days."

"Fine," she flopped her arms to her sides and gripped the gown in sweaty palms. "Make me into this nasty exterminating monster."

"It' ll be the both of us." He smiled.

"How? You hardly have the appetite for rats."

"No, but we' ve got to pull this off in a way that' s believable, at least to a medieval set of mind. We can' t simply walk into a village, have you change into a snakewoman and start chasing rats."

Now she was curious. "What' s your idea?"

"Have you ever heard of the ' Pied Piper' ?"

Furrowing her brows, she said, "Some kind of fairy tale about a guy leading rats somewhere?"

"Almost right. The Pied Piper played a flute and led the rats into a lake where they drowned." His forehead creased in thought. "There' s even a little ditty they wrote." His voice boomed when he said the words.

"In the year 1284 after the birth of Christ

From Hamelin were led away

One hundred thirty children, born at this place

Led away by a Piper into a mountain."

"How on earth did you remember that poem?"

"Wrote a book report on the Pied Piper when I was in junior high." He shrugged. "The poem just stuck."

"But the poem says nothing about him leading rats away."

He shrugged. "I know. The villagers didn' t pay his fee for all his hard work, so he got them back by stealing their children."

"Great, just when I was beginning to think there might be something noble in helping get rid of the rats."

Raynor laughed hard. "We' re not going to steal their children, even if they don' t pay us. And you' re right, it is a noble cause."

"How so?" she interrupted him.

"The fleas caused the Plague, and by killing rats, you' re essentially doing away with the source of disease infestation."

"You do make it sound so noble." This time she laughed. Her look turned serious just as swiftly, she asked, "Are we in the time period when the Black Plague was decimating Europe?"

Shaking his head in the negative, he said, "From talking to the townspeople, I found out it nearly wiped out their whole place some twenty years ago. Be glad we' re here now. It was horrendous according to the old man I spoke with."

"People scared to death, bodies piled up, a horrible stench in the air from the disease and burning bodies." At his surprised look, she replied, "I remember reading about it in high school."

"Unfortunately, it' s still around. They have small outbreaks occasionally."

"So, Pied Piper, how are you going to help me pull this off?" She frowned.

"We find a mark—" At her disapproving look, he corrected, "customer. Then, we go inside, you change and eat up all the rats you can find."

Folding her arms, she waited for his soliloquy to finish.

"I play a flute inside while you work, and then you bring me a few rodents to stick in a bag. The villagers see the bag outside and assume we' ve caught all the rats. Presto. A job well done, money exchanged for service rendered."

"You make it sound so simple—for you!" She picked up one of the exquisitely embroidered pillows and pounded it.

"Aw, Briana, she really doesn' t mind." He tried to touch her, but she jerked away.

"But I mind." By God, he had no idea how much she minded every time she was sucked into the snakewoman' s world.

"You' re the one who' s been complaining about not getting all your rights. Here' s your chance—you' ll be fulfilling a career position no other woman in this century can claim."

"Save your sarcasm and boyish charm. I' ll do it," she fumed, "because I want a change of clothing too." She tugged at the skirt of the dress; a ripping sound erupted. "Uh oh." She sighed and plucked at the tear. That was the final straw. She *had* to have a new change of clothing.

Briana abruptly remembered her simmering vegetables and ran to the brazier. They were fine and smelled pretty good too. Raynor grabbed two of the goblets and then speared the vegetables with his knife. He handed her a goblet, but she set it aside regretfully, letting it cool first. Smiling, he did the same, although he could have used the knife as a makeshift utensil.

"Plates and utensils are officially added to my next shopping trip."

"I don' t think they used utensils, just their fingers."

"Then, I' ll bring you back a knife." After a while, he picked up the goblet and dipped his fingers in, retrieving a cooked carrot. Plopping it into his mouth, he gave an exaggerated "yummy" sound.

Following his lead, she fingered out a carrot as well. A pleased expression came over her; it was scrumptious. Silence reigned as they ate hurriedly from the goblets. Of course he' d forgotten to buy salt, but the fresh vegetables were delicious anyway.

* * * * *

The next day they found the stream close to the castle ruins, as he' d promised. It was a nice-sized one, about five feet across, and they discovered one end had been dammed by a pile of brush and mud, forming a pool. For some reason, Raynor didn' t change into his new clothing and then turned to unlace her dress.

"Your chemise should do fine until you get your clothes washed."

He was right; the chemise was not made like the modern ones she was familiar with, it was short-sleeved, but more like a slip, reaching to her ankles. Shivering violently, she knew she' d just have to make do. Taking the bundle of clothes to the pool, she bit her lower lip and she stared at the material, not sure where to begin.

"Here, you'll need this." He handed her the soap. "I've seen TV programs where primitive people washed their clothes by beating them against rocks."

"I'm not going to beat a silk dress against rocks!"

Sorting through the clothes, she started with the thicker overdress, not sure just how much scrubbing she should do on any one piece. But, washing the less delicate pieces first, should give her a pretty good idea.

The process went much better than she'd have guessed; the homemade soap rid the material of all dirty spots and left them smelling clean.

Raynor helped her drape her things carefully over bushes. Luckily, he'd made a fire before they started. Thoroughly chilled by the time she finished scrubbing the clothes, she sat next to the campfire, wrapping the cloak around her. Wearing only a thin shirt was no defense against the chilly day, but it would have been difficult to bend over and launder with the cloak on to protect her.

Watching Raynor wash his clothes was interesting; he was very meticulous. His new purchases had included a new, better fitting tunic, but he'd not brought back a new undershirt. Ignoring the cold, he stripped his upper body and washed the male equivalent of a chemise, made like a shirt with short sleeves. His muscular chest was very nice, the ridged abs making his torso even more fascinating. The light trail of black hair across his chest didn't detract from his physique, and the sparse growth starting above his belly button and growing downward into his clothes drew her eyes to his groin. Unfortunately, he'd wrapped the new tunic around his waist as a cover and she was curious.

"Why the tunic cover?" she asked. "Afraid to show me your buns?" She couldn' t keep a giggle from escaping.

"Nope." He grinned at her. "Afraid the shock would be too much for you." He waved a hand at the leggings. "These things are made...crotchless."

"Oh," she blushed, mostly due to the sudden erotic image that conjured up. Of course she' d not had as much opportunity as she wished to get a good look at Raynor' s cock here in merry ol' England, since his clothes were ill-fitting and loose. And her memories while transformed into the snakewoman were fuzzy at best. From the one time she' d managed to make love to him in human form, she did remember its dark pink color, large size, and steely hardness. But she wanted to examine it in detail and know its individual curves, taste his unique flavor.

Flushing with heat, she recalled the large organ that had made itself known once Raynor had metamorphosed into the wolfman. It had been impressive. She idly watched him hang his clothes to dry, wishing she could see beneath the tunic around his waist, like some teenage girl desiring to get her first look at a man' s "thing". Briana giggled at her own silliness.

Thankfully, he didn' t hear her, but continued with his laundry chore. He was circumcised at least, something she cared more about than actual size. Of course she had nothing to worry about in that department; Raynor had a nice-sized cock.

"Jeez, it' s cold." Shivering, he rushed to the fire after he finished.

"I' m sorry." She came out of her sexual musings. "I should have helped you hang your clothes to dry."

"You seemed distracted." His voice was deep, his tone purposely sexy.

She realized he' d guessed her wayward thoughts by the mischievous look in his amber eyes and she blushed furiously.

"We could, uh, work on our bonding, if we weren' t exposed here." Raynor lowered his voice even further. Maybe he was hinting that they could make love once they returned to the tower. Clearly, it was too dangerous here, so she knew he wasn' t serious with his words, just suggestive.

Nodding absently, she silently cursed her inability to stay human. How she' d love to get her hands on him right this minute and run them all over that delicious body of his! A chill hit her. For a moment she was alarmed, but then realized it was simply the cold getting to her, perhaps the only thing standing between her and shifting. Raynor had certainly done his part, albeit innocently, in getting her senses stirred up.

They spent the afternoon snacking on the food from the pack, chatting, and turning the clothes so they' d dry faster. The clouds were heavy and the sun barely peeked out every once in a while, so the process of drying took a while. If it were not for the fact the bushes were ringed around the fire, she doubted they would have dried that day at all.

Eying the swiftly running stream, she asked, "Do you think we should bathe while we' re here?"

"Water' s too cold." He chuckled. "Besides, we really don' t need a bath."

"Huh?"

"Remember what I told you about less ' waste disposal' ?"

She threw her eyes skyward in response to his silly remark. "And the better mouth breath." She added.

"Exactly. Smell your underarm, you' ll see what I mean."

"I' ll take your word for it." She made a moue of disgust, and then sniffed her arm anyway. It smelled fresh.

He ran a hand through his long locks. "Your hair won' t feel dirty either." He paused when his hand became hung up in a tangle. "Although a brush will have to be added to my shopping list."

Running a hand through her short hair, Briana realized he was right. Her hair felt clean and it didn' t itch either. But her leg hairs were scratchy. "I wish you could add a razor to that list."

Grinning, he said, "Don' t I know it." He added, "Still, a hot shower would be great."

Making a sucking sound with her mouth, she said, "I know our breath is sweet because of the shifting, but my mouth feels yucky. I miss brushing." Of course crunching on apples did help, but it wasn' t enough tooth cleaning action to replace her toothbrush.

"Hmmm, I' ll see what I can do. I don' t think these folks were to up on dental hygiene."

"You know, there' s something I' ve been wondering about," she interrupted a quiet spell. "This time jumping, does it ever interfere with human history?"

Chapter Thirteen

Raynor gave her a serious look. "It can, that' s why we are trained before we leap. Taught to avoid shifting in front of humans, if at all possible, and to shun them until we get control over whatever type of shapeshifter we change into in the past."

"But…what if a shifter kills a human?" She knew his thoughts went to the vampires, just as hers had.

"If it is a shifter from that time period, for example if those vampires are from the medieval era, it makes little difference."

"Makes little difference!"

He smiled at her gently, "What I mean, if a human' s death is fated, it will happen, no matter the source. So, if one is killed by a shifter, it makes no difference in the historical perspective. The elders can sense if there' s a ' ripple' in the time fabric, an indication that a human was murdered by a shifter, when such was not fated to be. That' s what I meant by usually making little difference."

"That sounds so cold."

"It' s not as cold as you might think." He paused, "One of our most sacred teachings is not to harm humanity. We are more powerful than they. We could rule this planet if we wished, but that is not our way. We only wish to ' live in peace' as the old saying goes, study humans and their history."

Smiling tentatively, she asked, "What about jumpers, like us?"

Throwing a branch into the fire, he said, "That' s another story. As I said, we have to be very careful, or we could change human history."

"What about horrible creatures, like those vampires? Isn' t anything done about beasts like that?"

"As a matter of fact—"

"Ho," a familiar voice interrupted him. They turned and watched Robert' s spry figure run toward them.

"What do you do here, Robert?"

"Thought I' d try my luck at fishing and saw the fire." His glance took in the clothes lying across various bushes. "I see it' s wash day."

Raynor jumped up and ran his hands over her clothes, then gathered them and handed them to her. The boy had not noticed her undressed state since she had the cloak pulled about her. But once Raynor handed her the clothes, his eyes went to her bare ankles showing beneath the velvet and he blushed a dark pink.

Wiggling an eyebrow at her roguishly, Raynor clapped the boy on the shoulder and led him away while she re-dressed. She watched his broad back, admiring the way the cloth stretched across its width. Smoothing the front of the dress down, she idly wished they were alone, somewhere private. Then, she' d boldly slip it down; let the bodice hang on her breasts. She' d watch the heat swirl in his eyes as he took in her half-dressed state.

"Daydreaming?" His deep voice cut through her musings. Her response was a blush. She turned towards the wood so he wouldn' t see it. Coming up behind her, he laced her dress unobtrusively while the boy stirred the fire and threw on a few branches. She pictured his hands slipping beneath the material instead of lacing it. His hands sliding around, kneading her breasts, while the movement of the silk caressed her nipples into hard points.

A branch popped loudly, shaking her from her reverie. She realized Raynor' s observant eyes were glued to her face.

Turning to Robert, she asked, "We were going to eat some bread. Want a piece?" She offered the child a large chunk even while she asked. He accepted with a pleased smile.

"Are you a princess?" Robert asked out of the blue.

"Whatever made you ask that?" She laughed. "I hardly look like one."

The boy stared at her shyly. "You' re pretty enough…it' s just that you seem special."

Raynor and she stared at the boy in surprise. Did he have some kind of psychic powers? Could he sense her "specialness"?

His reference to a princess reminded her of her friend Eddie' s favorite story. Many times, they' d sat on her front porch while they took turns reading from the worn fairy tale book.

"I' m really not, but would you like to hear a story about a princess who didn' t appear to be a princess either?"

"Oh, yes please!" He clapped his hands in excitement.

Briana spent some few minutes telling him the story of Sleeping Beauty, embellishing it as much as her imagination could, especially the fight scenes, which she saw he enjoyed thoroughly.

After she finished, he jumped up and ran to the stream, but returned quickly. In his hand he held a bunch of daisies, which he shoved toward her.

"Thank you for the story."

Not to be outdone, Raynor recounted a tale of Robin and his men.

Standing up after his tale was complete, she remarked, "I' d better go start dinner."

"Do you mind going back alone?" He added, "Robert and I are going to try our hand at fishing."

Nodding, she watched a few minutes before leaving, pleased at the boy and man getting along in such a friendly way. Raynor had a kind heart, she saw, and seemed to like children as well.

Robert was tickled with the fishing items Raynor displayed. Apparently, he had no tackle and she wasn' t sure how he had planned on catching fish. Unless he was going to simply plunge into the icy water and try it by hand. The boy was shocked when Raynor attached the line to a sturdy pole and showed him how it worked. He didn' t seem to know about pole-fishing, which she found very interesting. Robert would have a new skill to share with his fellow villagers when he returned home.

* * * * *

Briana was shocked later when she stood in front of the mirror and saw how wrinkled the gown was. How was she going to go out in public like this? The next instant, she discarded that worry. Why should she care what these people thought of her? She was going to be leaving soon anyway.

The brazier had gone out hours ago and it was darn cold. Briana lay down on the soft bed and snuggled beneath the fur throw, disregarding the already hopelessly wrinkled condition of her dress. Warmth was more important than looks right now. Biting her bottom lip, she suddenly wondered just how much longer she was going to have to suffer in this difficult environment.

Merry ol' England was a tough old girl to get used to, especially for modern people. She and Raynor were going to have to work more diligently on bonding if they were to escape anytime soon. She played the images of his masculine chest through her mind, readying herself for his return. Soon, daydreams of a heated encounter with her handsome companion floated through her mind.

She remembered his skilled kisses with no problem and replayed them mentally for her own pleasure. Then, she recalled the tenderness with which he licked and suckled her breasts. She was toasty warm now, her own body providing much needed heat. Briana cupped her breasts beneath the cover and pressed gently while the image of Raynor licking them filled her thoughts and senses. Her nipples were hard. She tweaked and rolled them between her fingers while picturing him doing the same thing.

Her musings took on an exciting realism when she saw her own nude body, her legs splayed wide with Raynor kneeling between them. His eyes ran over her form, devoured and ignited it to cinders, while his amber orbs shone like tiny molten suns. The daydream Briana was much more bold than she could ever be; this side of her was comfortable with her exposed position, and needed no further urgings when he commanded her to open her lips…

Using both hands, she did as he requested, never taking her eyes from his face, receiving a heated coil of excitement from his hot eyes.

"Wider." His voice was rough.

Not sure which body parts he meant exactly, she spread her legs wider and then also pulled her flesh further apart.

"Yes," he breathed out a ragged response. "You' re so beautiful, so pink." Raynor' s eyes came back up to her face when he asked, "Will you taste as sweet as you look?"

Her stomach clenched in anticipation when his head dipped to her mons immediately after that statement-like question. No pretense of kissing his way down her belly, just an instant response. He rubbed his nose and face into her flesh, as if imprinting her scent into his own skin, and then followed with his tongue.

Warm, wet, and soft. Was there any other part of a man' s body that felt as wondrous? Briana had to smile at her own thoughts. His cock was just as good in its own right, but now she wanted to enjoy this particular offering. His skill was amazing. That beautiful appendage circled, swept up and down, and flicked her clit into a stew of excitement. Of course his lips were added into the mix, driving her up the side of a roller coaster ride sensation. Not at the top yet, but close.

A sudden wicked, inventive thought wedged itself into her musings. She vaguely remembered the snakewoman' s tongue and how it drove Raynor crazy. Following her command, the dream Raynor reared up and opened his mouth; his extremely long tongue snaked out. *Good*, she thought, *just as impressive as the snakewoman.* Now, she had him reposition himself between her thighs...

Closing her eyes, she used only her sense of feeling while his tongue slid slowly inside her vagina. Its magnificent length filled her completely, causing her to groan aloud. At first, he simply wiggled it back and forth, making her squirm. But then he began a dance of slow withdrawal and shoving it back in.

He changed the movements as it pleased him, or maybe he was picking up cues from her body and responding to them. Sometimes he plunged his tongue back in fast and furious, alternating it with the plodding motion. It was driving her crazy, just as she'd done him while in her snakewoman form. She was wet, as slippery inside as his tongue was.

Abruptly, he changed tactics again, withdrawing his tongue and flicking her clit quickly a few times before shoving it back inside her. Briana moaned loudly, her hips moving in a restless manner. Electric tingles shot through her clit and her whole pussy throbbed, felt swollen and achy. Opening her eyes, she panted in reaction to watching his black hair spill over her lower belly. Suddenly, he raised up slightly, as if sensing her observation and stared at her while his tongue continued its sensual shimmy.

Her head fell back onto the bed. She was quickly nearing the top of that coaster ride, her insides molten and her body trembling. She was truly being tongue-fucked. Raynor had increased the tempo of his movements. She reared up again, grabbed his head and dug her hands into his soft hair. Shoving her hips back and forth, she pressed his head more deeply into her soft tissues. "Oh, Raynor," she screamed. The orgasm that gripped her was huge and explosive. She screamed, her toes clenched in a tight ball, and she rode the aftershocks of sensation, her hands clutching his hair.

Exhaustion overcame her. Briana opened her eyes to a room empty of Raynor. She sighed. It had only been a daydream, albeit an awesome one. Her hands moved restlessly and she realized both had been pressed hard against her mons. Her clit throbbed unmercifully and she pushed down against it and rubbed several times. That was all it took for a real orgasm to grip her.

Her clit pulsated, and her vagina spasmed, as if Raynor' s cock were really inside her. Briana rode the experience, letting it consume her and groaning slightly in response. She lay some minutes, composing herself, before jumping up.

She was surprised when she discovered the wetness beneath her. Tearing a small piece of her chemise, she wetted it and wiped herself. Jeez what an experience! These dreams of hers were becoming hotter and hotter. Would the reality of her and Raynor' s lovemaking in human form match her dream sequence? She smiled to herself. Of course he couldn' t grow a tongue like the snakewoman, but if he had expertise in that area, he could be almost as effective as the dream Raynor without it.

* * * * *

When he came back hours later, she' d lost interest in a sexual liaison. Laundering outside in less than perfect circumstances had drained her energy, the orgasm had added to her tiredness, and her throat felt raw. Two large fish were tied to a piece of the fishing line, which he carried proudly. She' d already started the fire and Raynor placed the fish carefully over the coals.

"You were gone a long time. Were the fish not biting?"

"Yes." He waved toward the brazier. "Caught four more. I gave Robert two."

Raising her eyebrows in surprise, she asked curiously, "What about the other two?"

"I walked the boy home, and he told me about this friend of his who owns a flute. So, he took me to his cottage and we worked out a deal."

"Two fish for a flute? Is that a good deal?"

Grinning, he pulled out the aforementioned instrument. "It's hand-carved, kind of rough-looking, but it works." He put the flute to his lips and played "ring around the rosies". It was crude, but recognizable. At her look, he said, "Been a while, I played clarinet in high school."

"Oh." She stared at the slowly cooking fish. "You know what you were saying about not changing history…I was wondering about you showing Robert how to fish with a pole. Wouldn't you be changing history by introducing something these people don't know about yet?"

"Uh, well, it's just a small thing."

His uncomfortable expression told her he wasn't too sure about that statement. The next instant, he snapped his fingers. "Robert told me it is a known method, but no one in his village has ever tried it. They think pole-fishing is for people of leisure—meaning the rich."

"How did he intend to catch fish before he ran into us?"

"His people string lines with several hooks on them, that way they can catch more than one fish at a time."

"Trotline fishing," she said. At his quizzical look, she explained, "A traditional way of fishing for good ol' boys in the South."

Staring into the red coals for a minute, he said, "You're right though, I need to be careful."

She wondered if he felt guilty about what he' d done. It had ended up okay, but it could have been otherwise.

He glanced up at her. "The quicker we bond, the sooner we can go home."

How long did he really think it would take? His brow wrinkled as he peered at her; he seemed to notice her drawn features.

"Are you okay?" He was concerned; his tone of voice proved that.

"Tired and my throat is raw."

"Probably the cold outside."

Nodding, she asked, "Do you think I' m catching a cold?"

Chuckling, he said, "Have you ever had a cold in your life?"

"No." Then she remembered what he' d said about shifters not catching human diseases. "I' ve never had anything but cuts and bruises."

She became lost in her own thoughts while Raynor concentrated on the fish. She remembered the time she' d fallen off the roof when she was six. Of course she shouldn' t have crawled out the attic window onto the roof, but she' d only suffered a purple bruise on one shin. It had disappeared completely in two days. No one but her parents knew about her injury, and they ignored it after checking for broken bones.

Other occasions came to mind, when she' d cut or bruised herself in play and quickly healed. She was surprised when Raynor called her over to eat.

He had speared the fish with his knife and placed them into the pot. The smell was mouth-wateringly good and she could barely wait for it to cool before tearing into the succulent meat.

"What kind of fish is this?" she asked between bites.

"Perch."

"I thought perch were small?"

"These are fairly big, as far as perch go, but not a rarity even in our time. Maybe a pollution-free environment helps the fish grow larger."

She'd scraped and chopped a handful of raw vegetables earlier, and they complimented the fish dinner well. Afterwards, they talked for a while before going to bed, although it was mostly Raynor sharing his fishing experience with Robert. Too tired to chat, she listened, only contributing one remark: "I hope I have a son like Robert one day."

"He is a sweet kid, isn' t he?" Raynor snuggled her beneath his chin and yawned. "Sounds like a pretty good wish to me."

* * * * *

That night she slept solidly, waking the next morning feeling refreshed, and her throat was fine.

Getting dressed and eating was a rushed affair as usual, with the chill air hurrying them on. "What' s on the agenda today?" she asked curiously. Raynor had that look, like he had a goal in mind.

Picking up the flute, he waved it in the air. "Exterminating."

She groaned but followed him anyway. "Where are we going?"

"Robert told me there' s a wealthy family who live about a mile past his village." He stared down at her shoes. "I thought you could make it that far in those."

She did, but her feet were aching by the time they approached the large manor house. Wrapping the cloak around her form, she covered her wrinkled dress. It wouldn' t help their cause if the people thought they were vagrants. Briana waited outside while Raynor spoke with the owner. After a short while, a richly dressed couple exited, followed by several children and a multitude of servants. Raynor waved her to follow him inside.

The couple stared at her curiously when she passed, but nodded politely. "What did you tell them?" she asked once the door was closed.

"That I have the skill of the Pied Piper and that you assist me by holding the bag. I did have to jog their memory about the Piper, since it' s apparently not a widely known story yet."

"And they believed you?"

"They believe in the Pied Piper." He paused and grinned. "The man didn' t particularly care if he has rats running about, but the wife does. Plus, I added a little garnish."

"What?"

"Told them my grandmother was a great healer and she always thought rats were the cause of the Plague. That got their attention." Turning her about, he untied her dress, and then pointed to a majestic gothic chair in the great hall. "I' ll wait here until you' re finished."

She walked into the next room, not wanting to strip in front of him, and not crazy about shifting before his eyes either. Rustling, scurrying sounds were easy to detect. She' d have no problem shifting; the snakewoman reacted swiftly to her prey.

* * * * *

"Don' t forget to save me a few," he called after she slithered pass him some time later. The sound of several different merry tunes filled the house while she worked.

The snakewoman returned after thirty minutes and plopped the squirming rat she clutched in her tongue, into the bag he held out. Moving swiftly into the next room, she made two return trips to dump rats into the bag. Disappearing into the room once again, she returned a few minutes later in human form, then turned her back and waited for him to lace her up.

When they exited, the grouped people had curious looks on their faces, the man a suspicious one. Raynor held up the bag. He' d stuffed it earlier with leaves, so that the rats squealing and bumping against the sides appeared to be more rats than the actual number.

"How many did you catch?" The man' s voice was still suspicious, but his expression less so.

Raynor glanced to her. "A dozen," she replied quickly.

"That' s three pence a head, as agreed."

"Highway robbery! Besides, how do I know you caught a dozen?" The man' s eyes had a merchant' s gleam to them; she could imagine him doing accounting in his head.

Shrugging, Raynor said, "I can dump them back inside, if you wish?"

"No!" The wife screamed and stepped in front of her husband. Turning to him, she stated firmly, "Pay them."

Looking sheepish, the man dug into his money bag and handed them the correct coins.

Briana felt very good when they walked away. Even her sore feet didn' t deter her elation when they reached the tower again.

* * * * *

She was in an even better mood when Raynor took off early the next morning for the town. The afternoon had arrived by the time he returned and she greeted him eagerly.

He unwrapped the bundle and spread the goods out. Grabbing the dress on top, she spread it out for a better view. It was lovely, but immensely more practical than the silk dress she wore. The material was a very soft wool, the color a beautiful golden-brown. Such fine fabric wouldn' t be itchy like poor Raynor' s coarsely-made tunic. The shopkeeper had supplied a sleeveless chemise, which would keep the wool from lying directly against her skin. At least that gave her two chemises, so she could wash one while wearing the other.

"I told the lady you were a few inches taller than you are."

"Huh?"

"That way, the dress shouldn' t drag the ground. I noticed this is a problem for you."

"That was smart," she remarked, thinking how kind it had been also. Turning her back to him, she waited for the unlacing. "I' ll be back," she said over her shoulder when she headed for the curtains around the bed.

"Don' t you want to see what else I brought?"

Chapter Fourteen

"In a bit." After getting dressed in the new gown, she was in a much better mood. The material hit her just above the ankles and made walking so much easier.

When she came out from behind the bed drapes she'd pulled closed he held out a small pair of soft leather boots. Taking them gratefully, she slipped off the shoes with wooden soles. The boots fit very well—they hit her at the ankle.

He'd arranged the items on the table. Looking over the collection, Briana was pleased with the items he'd bought, which included two wooden plates, a knife for her, and a hairbrush. Two small pieces of cloth and a pile of green leaves intrigued her. "What are these?"

He took the material from her. "I thought maybe I could wrap these around sturdy branches." At her questioning look, he added, "Makeshift toothbrushes."

"Oh." She stirred the leaves with a finger. "And these?"

"They're mint leaves. We could make mint tea. But I thought we could crush them and make our own toothpaste."

Leaning down, she took a deep breath of the fragrant leaves. "You're a genius."

He blushed, a pleased expression lighting his handsome face. "I just remembered how much I like my mint toothpaste."

Grabbing his arm, she said, "I was so excited over the dress, I forgot about the underclothes."

"Underclothes?" He gave her a sidelong glance and then blushed. "The shopkeeper looked at me like I was crazy when I asked...well, first I had to explain what underwear was." He chuckled. "They don' t wear underclothes in this century, but luckily the lady thought I was from France."

Folding her arms, she gave him an agitated look, but then relented; he' d done well with the dress and boots. "I' ll just have to make do." His look was still slightly wary and she thought perhaps she' d been a bit ungracious. "Thank you." She stood on tiptoe and planted a kiss on his cheek. Well, she tried to, but he turned just when she reached his face and they ended up involved in a full frontal smack.

Raynor' s lips pressed against hers when she tried to withdraw, and then unexpectedly, she didn' t want to. The kiss was electrifying; perhaps it was the spontaneity. Her nipples hardened when their mouths adjusted for fuller penetration and their tongues came into play. Both his hands were gripping her shoulders gently. She ran her hands over his and then moved them down to her excited breasts, arching backwards while he slowly kneaded them.

The still unlaced dress slipped down her body, aided by her wiggling and his hands. The next instant she was shoving at his tunic and it was flung across the room after he tugged it off quickly. Their lips reattached, as if strong magnets were glued between them, pulling them forcefully together.

His arms slid over her hips then gripped her upper thighs. Briana held her breath in anticipation when Raynor lifted her. She swiftly locked her legs around his waist. He eased her down gently. She slid with no problem onto his cock, her slick fluids making it a passage of little effort. She clutched his neck and stared into his brilliant amber eyes when he moved her butt up and down. Closing her eyes, she allowed the sensation of erotic awareness alone to invade her body. Her vagina was full, stretched to its limit, yet was a greedy bitch and demanded more.

Wriggling around on him in this position was difficult, but still exciting. It took a strong man to make love in the standing position. That thought made her wet. Giving her a quick peck on the lips, Raynor took a firm hold on her and began walking toward the bed. Once there he lowered her carefully, then stretched out on top of her. Briana's hands ran up and down his muscular biceps, wondering at the power in them. She loved the feel of his heavy weight on top of her while they moved together.

He was simply watching her while slowly moving his cock in and out, as if he too were soaking up her response. Grabbing his head on either side, she brought his lips down to her with haste, eager to continue their oral assault. She groaned into his mouth, taken once again by his expertise and the unique fruity flavor that pervaded her senses.

He was going to drive her up the wall with the slow sensual dance he performed. Withdrawing probably half-way, he pushed in slowly and then drew back just as agonizingly slowly, repeating it over and over while her vagina pulsated. Her body clenched and then went limp; her lower lips ached for him, invited him further inside with upward motions of her hips. She wanted all of him jammed inside her soft, liquid-filled walls, yet didn't want his drive-me-crazy movements to stop either.

"Oh, yes," she moaned into his lips, rotating her hips wildly, bucking up to meet his thrusts.

"Tell me what you want," he whispered against her lips, causing a thrumming sensation in them.

"I want you to make love to me," she answered without hesitation, not wishing him to stop for even a minute.

His movements became full strokes, his cock plunging into her with masculine force now. Sucking her lower lip into his mouth and doing maddening things to it with his teeth and lips. He let it drop and whispered while he posed just above her lip. "What else to you want?"

She wasn' t sure exactly where he was going with this seduction, but her tongue came out and licked his lower lip, trying desperately to encourage him to continue. He withdrew a space, his hot stare washing over her face and then attaching itself to her eyes. A fiery sexual need was reflected in those amber depths, but also something else — something born of the human need for affection. Briana didn' t know how she knew this, but she did.

His strokes had slowed again, doing that agonizing cock dance that drove her nearly over the edge.

Grasping his hair, she brought him to within kissing distance again, whispering her answer against his sexy lower lip, "I want you."

His lips descended on her with a conquering forcefulness and she opened her mouth wider. She loved washing her emotions in the sensation of someone else taking complete control of her body and thoughts, even if but for a short spell. They both groaned when he again took up the sensual dance.

She paused in their kiss, her eyes widening in awakening knowledge when the spasms hit her mid torso. No moaned protests left her mouth; only her eyes spoke her disappointment when the snakewoman took over her body.

Raynor had hoped he could bring his lovely Briana to orgasm before his sultry snake goddess made her appearance, but it wasn' t to be. When she started her wild movements upon his cock, he became distracted from any thoughts but her frenzied movements.

He shifted in reaction to her primitive actions. The sudden urge to bite her soft flesh hit him and he peered into her hypnotic eyes, voicing his unspoken need. Snake goddess had an uncanny way of knowing his desires. But, this time he also saw a raw need reflected in her green-slitted orbs, only he wasn' t so good at guessing her wishes.

"What is it you desire?" he asked, his voice low-toned and hoarse. It was hard to speak when she ravaged his cock.

"To taste your skin, as you wish to do mine."

His eyes were drawn to her lush lips. Even while he looked, she slid her mouth open and relaxed her deadly three inch fangs into striking position, but then simply looked at him with a questioning stare. Could he? Dare he? The next question he asked himself was why would he? He answered that easy enough; he knew the sexual sizzle that ignited within himself when his fangs sank into her succulent flesh, the snake goddess desired the same experience.

"What about your venom?"

"I can withhold it."

Her peridot eyes were expectant and curious. He knew she wondered if he trusted her enough to allow such liberties. And he did. He did not wish to withhold from her an experience he'd desired himself and wished to repeat.

Rising to his knees, he turned his head, exposing his left side. Gracefully, she flowed to her knees in front of him.

He couldn't help it—he held his breath while her head moved slowly toward his shoulder. But then she moved with eye-blinking speed, so that the pain of her sharp, long fangs striking was less intense than he guessed it would have been if she'd sunk them in slowly. She'd chosen the area between his neck and shoulder joint, probably because it was less sensitive then the neck. For this consideration, he was thankful. As it was, sharp needles of pain shot from the two pinpricks.

Turning his neck slowly, he held in the gasp while pain lanced through his upper body. Sinking his fangs into her exposed neck took but a heartbeat. The pain that throbbed through his head and shoulders began to subside while he drank in slowly from her strong shapeshifter blood.

She hadn't moved a micrometer the whole time. She seemed to realized it would cause him further pain. Now, her tongue began a gentle caress between her fangs, soothing his skin. It wiggled down his back, came back up to stroke his neck and upper shoulder. Raynor wondered if her saliva had healing properties, because abruptly all pain stopped as if it'd never been.

Acting in kind, he smoothed his tongue between his fangs and received a shiver of excitement from his beautiful snake goddess. Remembering they were locked in a lover's embrace, he began to move slowly in and out of her mysterious channel again. He had stayed hard through the whole process, something he found somewhat surprising due to the intense pain when she first sank her fangs into him.

Suddenly, his whole system was galvanized with pleasure so acute, it almost seemed as if the pain of her fangs sinking into his shoulder had returned. But it was a deep, thrilling sexual humming along his veins, not torment from physical injury. He began thrusting again while he sucked her blood into his throat, and his lower body reacted with wild thrusts that were matched with maddening intensity by his partner.

She moaned between her fangs, making his skin between those sharp canines tingle. And he knew that she was experiencing the same hard-driven sexual need as he was. He needed her for sustenance — of his vampire thirst, of his soul seeking its soulmate, and of his male body striving for an orgasm to out blast any other before it.

Her strange alien thoughts crawled around the fringes of his mind and he welcomed them, took succor from them like another life-giving fluid. He threw his own sensual desires at her and heard her groan in his mind. Then she hissed aloud. A hiss of dark desire and need.

Warm blood flowed slowly over his tongue while her feminine fluids dripped from her slit and flowed down his cock, making it easier to thrust harder and deeper into her snake pussy. An invisible string of dark hunger sprang up between his mouth and his cock; he couldn't tell which was which. Was he fucking her neck or sucking blood from her secret feminine parts? It all ran together in a mind-blowing experience, one that ended in an orgasm that gripped his balls in a tight clench and rippled his body with spasms.

He bellowed while his hands grasped her slim waist until they dug into her yielding flesh. Her orgasm contracted around his cock, milking the last drops of his seed inside her channel, and she hissed loudly against his shoulder. She withdrew her fangs while the last of his intense climax flushed through his system, and he drew his sharp canines from her neck as well. He rested his head against her shoulder, breathing deeply while her tongue laved the puncture area, making it numb and cool at the same time.

Barely having the strength to lift his head, he nevertheless licked her neck where his fangs had penetrated. They fell ungracefully to the mattress, both spent beyond belief. After some minutes, while they cuddled, they shifted.

"When do I get to go to town?" she asked abruptly.

"Soon."

"How about tomorrow?"

"Tomorrow...I just got back today," he groaned, but then saw her face and smiled. "Okay, tomorrow.

* * * * *

The walk to the township wasn' t bad. It felt wonderful to stretch her legs, and the boots were comfortable. Several people waved and greeted Raynor once they arrived. There appeared to be one main street, which was narrow, with quaint shops and cottages lining it. They were jammed in next to each other. Most were two story structures, unlike the simple one story dwellings of the villagers. Some were made of stone, but most from wood. Like the smaller village, some abodes looked dismally empty.

Shops were located in the center of the town, and many people strolled along, either window-shopping or purchasing items from inside the charming places.

"I' m surprised the town is so crowded with people." Her eyes flicked over the boarded up homes.

"I think a lot of people come from the nearby villages for market day and to shop."

Briana shook her head in agreement; it was a reasonable assumption. Pushing aside her disturbing thoughts about the many people who had died of the Plaque for it to be so empty, she enjoyed browsing leisurely through a fabric shop. The many choices surprised her. Silk, velvet, brocade, linen, and various types of wool were offered for sale.

"You' d look beautiful wrapped in this." Raynor pulled down a swatch of silken red material from a tall shelf.

Her hand smoothed over the fabric, enjoyed its luxurious texture. She' d never thought much of silk before; it seemed too delicate for a career woman' s wardrobe. But the soft, erotic feel of it as it slid over her hands, entranced her. Maybe she could consider silk eveningwear, or a nightgown made of its rich fabric. "When we get back, I might buy an outfit made of silk."

"Sounds good. But you look better with nothing but your hair covering you."

Not thinking, she answered, "My hair is not long enough to cover anything." Her hand paused as it fingered blue silk and she glanced at him.

Raynor was grinning ear to ear. She felt the dark blush creep up her neck and burn her cheeks.

Exiting the shop swiftly, she halted when she spied a pub, from which singing and jolly voices emitted. Peeking inside, she saw immediately it was not an establishment that welcomed women. But, a few minutes later, they ran across a vendor selling ale from his wagon. It was delicious and refreshing.

"Good."

She nodded her agreement. "Do you drink?"

"Only socially." He smiled at her and took another sip.

Happiness flashed through her at his answer. One of her boyfriends had been an alcoholic, and she'd promised herself she would never put up with another man who drank too much.

Pausing at a blacksmith's, they watched him shoe a horse. It was hot, hard work and Briana admired the man's diligence. The odor of horse manure and fresh hay was strong; conflicting smells of pleasant and not so pleasant. In fact, she realized, the whole town was pervaded by a stench. Unwashed bodies, the open stables, and pigs running underfoot, all vied for the most foul smelling award. Topping them all, was an open drainage ditch that ran along each side of the street, and more than once they had to sidestep while water and trash was thrown from windows to the ditch below.

Thankfully, a baker's shop invited them in with the delicious smells floating outside, covering the not so pleasant odors of the crowded town. They purchased a pastry apiece and then went outside, nibbling the goodies up. "Mmm." Briana swiped at a glob of jelly on her lower lip.

"Here, let me help." Raynor flicked the remaining dollop from her lip and stuck his finger in his mouth. He sucked on it noisily and grinned at her.

Briana' s stomach boiled and her nipples hardened instantly. It was as if he' d sampled her nipples instead of pastry jelly; at least, that' s what her wandering mind thought.

She noticed he had a crumb at the corner of his molded male lips. Reaching up, she brushed it away, but before she could move her finger, he grabbed it and licked the tip.

His charming smile and teasing lick caused heat to lash through her lower lips. Her clit jumped, as if he' d flicked it instead of her finger. She was sorry when he withdrew his tongue, taking her hand and walking on. But she knew they' d have time for sex later.

Spying a barbershop, they watched in fascination when leeches were applied to a man' s arm. When he got through with his medical duties, the barber cut another patron' s hair. The open market was the most enjoyable; almost anything you could imagine, at least in these times, were for sale. They didn' t return to the tower until late, just before sunset.

* * * * *

Raynor paused just inside the drawbridge. "I smell blood."

She hesitated but a few seconds before following him to the other tower, and screeched to a halt to keep from running into him. Raynor stood as rigid as a statue.

Peering around his shoulder, she gasped. There was a nude girl tied to the dining table and a very pale young man roped to the gothic chair.

Raynor strode to the table, anger evident in every step. Not wanting to see, but knowing she had to, Briana edged next to him.

The girl's wrists and ankles were tied by the ropes to each corner of the heavy table. Her white skin was marred by pinprick marks, not only on her neck and wrists, but also along her upper thighs. Dried blood had trickled from the wounds and pooled in small spots on the wood. Her eyes were drawn unwillingly to the young woman's lower body, where a larger splattering of blood was gathered between her thighs.

She blinked. For a second she wondered if they'd bitten the girl's tender female parts; such a thought made her shudder in sympathy. But then she realized they'd probably raped the poor thing.

Making them both jump, the girl opened her eyes and spoke, "I'm so cold."

"She's alive," Briana whispered, touching her hand and perceiving the barest of pulses.

Raynor jerked the tunic from his body and laid it gently around the girl's chest. "Who did this to you?" he asked, even though they were both quite sure who had perpetrated this horrible crime.

Her smooth brow wrinkled. "Thomas and I were paid good wages to bring fresh rushes to this room." Her lovely blue eyes caught Briana's tearful ones. "We were terrified to come here, but it was such good money."

Silence followed when her eyes closed, and Raynor shook her slightly. Her eyes came up to him this time. "I thought we did a good job; the floor was in a filthy state."

"Yes," she said softly, stroking the girl' s forehead. "You both did a lovely job." She turned the girl' s face toward her. "Can you tell us who injured you?"

Suddenly, the girl' s eyes widened in fear. She seemed to come out of her blood-loss haze. Her breath came in small, heaving pants and her lips trembled. She appeared to struggle mightily to speak. Raynor leaned down, but when he raised back up Briana knew the girl had died, even before he shook his head slowly, sadness lighting his golden eyes.

"Oh-h." The word stuck in her throat. She turned and quickly walked to the young man. Raynor had reached her side by the time she pressed two fingers against his neck. She straightened and shook her head as he' d done with the girl.

They stared down at the havoc wreaked on the man, barely past boyhood. He too had been bitten in the neck, wrists, and thighs. She had a sudden sickening image — that of the women vampires feasting on the young man and the male vampires on the girl.

"What do we do?" Fright, anger and nausea were wrapped up in one tight ball in her stomach.

"Kill them!" His statement was short, to the point, and she knew he meant it.

"But, we are only two against four." He simply stared at her, his anger barely held in check behind those amber orbs.

Ignoring her, Raynor untied the ropes on the young man — his body didn' t move, his limbs rested on the chair arms, while his handsome face drooped upon his chest. Returning to the table, Raynor undid the ropes binding the girl. He froze when his eyes traveled up from the wood top. Wondering what on Earth he could find to stun him after these grisly discoveries, Briana looked across the room, at floor level.

No, her mind denied it. It couldn' t be. She stumbled toward the small, crumpled body and Raynor reached for her, but his hands missed. Falling to her knees, she ignored the pain from hitting the cold earthen floor, and brushed a lock of brown hair from the staring eyes.

It was Robert. His sweet eyes would see no more…he was dead. Would she ever forget the look in those rigid eyes, one of horror and childish nightmares come true?

She doubted it. Gently turning his jaw towards her, then away, she was thankful for one tiny fact; there was only one vampire bite on his neck. The poor child had not had to suffer innumerable bites on his body. With his small size, she only hoped he' d died quickly.

Gathering him in her arms, she cradled his body like a mother for a long time, rocking gently, while tears streamed down her chin onto her bosom. Raynor stood behind her, offering comfort with his solid presence.

Finally, she stood, struggling with his limp weight, but thrusting off her companion' s attempt to help. "We must take him home to his father."

"Of course."

She faced him and stared into his eyes, hers hardened with resolve. "Whatever it takes." She could read by his expression that he understood, and he nodded his head in silent agreement. She was no longer terrified; she was past that, her grief turned inward into anger so intense, she wanted to strike out, rend the perpetrators into tiny bits of flesh.

"Look what we have here, visitors."

Just the voices she wanted, needed to hear.

"Why would you do this?" Raynor's voice was filled with anger.

The vampire they assumed was William of Haworth, stepped forward. "We told you already this is our play room...if we'd known you wished to participate in our games, we would have waited for you."

Briana sneered at his attempt at wit, and then gently laid Robert's body on the table next to the girl.

William's eyes flicked to her and he commented, "Can you believe that boy thought there was treasure hidden in these ruins?"

Raynor growled, and she knew his inner pain when he recalled his carefree remark to Robert concerning buried treasure. He shifted; it seemed to only take a few seconds, and she wondered if it was his anger and guilt fueling the swift change. The leader started toward him and the others appeared distracted by the two opponents.

Briana let her pain and anger swell inside until a lance of agony shot through her; she rode the process, welcomed it. She knew when the shift was complete, because she received that "distancing" effect when the snakewoman took over her senses. The vampires hissed and backed up, except for the leader who grappled with Raynor.

Ripping the now ill-fitting clothes from her, Briana/snakewoman advanced on the three vampires moving with whipcord speed to slam the door shut when the redhead female edged toward the exit. The vampire screamed and scuttled backward, bumping into the blonde woman.

The other male chose the less dangerous adversary and attacked Raynor from the back. She had no time to worry about her lover. He was strong, and she had two disgusting creatures to dispose of.

The flame haired vampire turned tail and cowered behind the chair holding the youth. Briana' s piercing stare caught the other. Her prey' s eyes were terrified, but defiant. The vamp jumped, intending to wrap her arms about the snakewoman' s throat, but Briana stretched upward and the woman' s hands flailed uselessly against her lower body.

Unexpectedly, the vampire drew her lips back and sank her fangs into Briana' s tail. The creature sucked mightily and by her expression, thought she' d gotten into an advantageous position. Snakewoman bent over, towering above the kneeling vampire. The shifter sensed her presence and glanced up, withdrawing her teeth in sudden fear. Briana crouched over her like a tigress, her long fangs exposed to their full lethal length.

With a loud hiss, she grabbed the vampire' s shoulders and hauled her upward, extending to her impressive seven foot height balanced on her tail. The woman paled to an icy white shade, her lovely blue eyes widening in horror at the fearful creature holding her in its iron-hard grasp.

In the meantime, Raynor was in the fight of his life. William was powerful, and they' d gotten in equal exchange of blows. The other male vampire jumped him from the back, but sweeping his arm backward with force, he knocked the fellow to the floor. While that one appeared momentarily stunned, Raynor let loose with a barrage of pummels to William's stomach.

Stumbling backward, the leader paused to catch his breath, and he took the opportunity to quickly check on Briana. By God, she was magnificent! The blonde vampire was being held above the floor like a wiggling morsel of food, ready for the snake goddess to devour. Her short hair stood out, like it was electric-charged, giving her the appearance of a hooded cobra. He didn't have time to let his thoughts wander further; William pounced on him again and he heard stealthy footsteps behind him.

The snakewoman shook the nasty creature in her grasp until her eyes practically popped from her head. Then, moving in agonizingly slow motion, she drew her into a tight embrace and bent her neck to the side. Drawing her lips back to their fullest, she stared into the vampire's terrified face just before sinking her fangs into her shoulder.

Briana/snakewoman did not suck blood into her mouth like the female vamp had done; instead she pumped venom from her impressive canines into the shifter. The woman struggled feebly for a few seconds, but then her body slumped when the poison hit her system, paralyzing her. Only then did she lower the blonde to the ground and stretch her out along the cold earth. Slithering over her form like a lover, the snakewoman took her time and pumped minute sluices of venom into the bites she ejected along the vampire's entire body.

The vamp's vocal cords were not affected because she'd bitten below the neck only, and behind the snakewoman's eyes, Briana got much satisfaction from the female's suffering. Little whimpers escaped the vampire's pale lips every time she bit deeply into a new fleshy spot. She saved the most sensitive areas for last, posing for a heartbeat over the blonde' s groin and staring with wicked snake eyes at her powerless victim.

Chapter Fifteen

The woman' s eyes bulged with fear and her breathing came in short pants, all she was capable of with the venom running through her system. Extending her long tongue, Briana wet the targeted path, great satisfaction welling up inside her at the deepening terror she read in the vampire' s eyes. Was that disgust she read also? Did the woman actually think she would lower herself to taste of such an offensive creature?

Chuckling out loud, she posed over her body, alternately licking the vamp' s thighs and then blowing on the wet spots gently. Her victim couldn' t move, but her skin prickled with goose bumps of terror. Too bad she couldn' t watch while Briana sank her fangs into her, but then maybe not seeing was even more horrifying.

Snakewoman dug her fangs slowly into the soft flesh at the woman' s thigh, just below her sex. A low sigh was pulled from the woman, sounding almost like a lover' s response, but far from it in truth. Inching her teeth in micrometers at a time, she extended the vampire' s torture, happy with the groans emitting from the still figure.

A sudden furtive movement drew her attention; the redheaded vampire was sneaking toward the door. Whipping off the woman with snake speed, she swayed in front of the exit when the vamp screeched to a stop. Panting in terror, the more timid female ran back and hid behind the huge chair again.

Shrugging her slim shoulders, Briana/snakewoman flowed back to her victim, highly disappointed when she saw the woman had stopped breathing. She turned toward the other female, but paused briefly to watch Raynor, who was holding his own against the two males. Then, she lowered her whole body to the floor and slithered in an exaggerated fashion toward the horrified female vampire.

Striking at one side of the chair with her tongue, she got the intended effect when the vampire ran from behind the chair on the other side. Snakewoman followed on her heels, and then slid in front of her in eye-blink speed. The female stood frozen; no paralyzing venom would be needed with this one.

Swaying gently, she considered how to make the redhead suffer. Suddenly remembering the vamp' s intense horror when she had swallowed a rat, Snakewoman smiled. Lowering her body, Snakewoman stared eye-to-eye with the shifter. Her terror was so much more evident than the other' s; she sent off a sweaty, palpable odor of fear.

Extending her tongue, she swiftly wrapped it around one of the female' s arms, and then pulled it slowly, inch by inch toward her mouth. When the tongue-encased hand entered her mouth, the woman started trembling so fiercely, she looked as if she were on the point of shifting, but she didn' t.

Briana/snakewoman wasn' t sure if she could do what she wanted to attempt, but she shrugged inwardly and decided to give it a shot anyway. Something in her snake senses knew what to do; her jaw unhinged, allowing her to open her mouth wider. Her throat muscles worked, tugging the hand, and then the arm gently down her throat.

When she reached the end of that arm and they were eyeball to eyeball, it was Briana who took control and stopped the process. The vampire had fainted dead away anyway. But, there was also a deep craving inside the snakewoman she found extremely disturbing, one Briana couldn' t allow her to fulfill and live with herself later.

Spitting out the arm took a little more effort, but she waited patiently afterwards for the woman to regain consciousness. When the vampire flapped her eyes open feebly, the gentler side of her, the part that was still Briana, felt sorry for the redhead—just enough that the snakewoman followed her inner urgings, finishing her off quickly. One bite to the neck and a powerful release of her venom ended the vampire' s mental torture.

Flowing up to her full height after her enemy' s demise, she watched her lover fight. He was a splendid shifter, a sexy vampire, and an excellent fighter. But right now, those vampire abilities were coming into play, aiding in his battle. Raynor' s teeth were sunk into the leader' s shoulder and his enemy threw his head back in agony while her lover drank deeply.

But, then the next instant he seemed to recover and sank his fangs into Raynor' s shoulder. Both men jerked loose, as if by mutual agreement. Back and forth they went across the room, as each hit each other with powerful blows from their fists. They rammed into the heavy table, tipping it up slightly in their struggle.

The other male vampire had been crouching against the wall, as if fearful of joining the fray, but he suddenly jumped on Raynor' s back, sinking his teeth into his neck. This was too much. Moving swiftly, she came up behind the smaller vampire and hissed next to his head.

He withdrew his fangs in surprise and she flipped him off quickly. He lay quietly, staring up at her in fear. When he made a move, she slithered closer and extended her fangs to their fullest. Lying back down, he did as she, watched the combatants.

The large men fought with almost superhuman strength. Thankfully, she noted that Raynor seemed to have better technique in boxing than his opponent. Soon, the leader began to tire and her lover killed him quickly, coming up behind him and breaking his neck.

Backing off slightly, she watched with satisfaction while Raynor towered over the downed vampire, who looked up at him with fatalistic acceptance. Another neck snapped and the last vampire lay dead.

After a few seconds of looking around at the carnage, he waved for her to follow him outside. They sat down on a lush green carpeting of grass, letting the peace and tranquility soak into them, until they began to shift.

"Are you okay?" the completely human Raynor asked her gently.

"Fine." She ran one hand down her thigh, glad to have legs again.

"What I could see of your fight, you were magnificent," Raynor said softly, admiration in his tone.

Her eyes dipped downward; shame and guilt washing through her. "And savage."

"Yes, but you had a just cause."

"You' re right." Her head came back up. There was no need to feel anything but satisfaction at the outcome of the battle.

After some time, he jumped to his feet and ran back inside, returning with her gown and chemise. Briana was astounded at herself; she'd completely forgotten she was nude.

Raynor watched a bird in the trees while she dressed. The chemise, dress, and overdress were torn; they'd have to be repaired later. He managed to tie the laces in a haphazard manner. The fit would be uncomfortable, but the clothes were wearable. When she finished dressing, he turned and went back through the doorway; she followed.

"What do we do with the bodies?"

Raynor looked around at the carnage. "This is going to be pretty hard to cover up." He rubbed his chin thoughtfully. "We can't let anyone discover the shifters' remains."

The four had died as vampires, their signature fangs were still very evident. "They don't shift back?'

"No," he shook his head. "Whatever form a shifter dies in, they stay that way." He stared at the tower. "I guess we bury them," he sighed. "That's going to be a lot of work for such scum."

"Scum," she repeated softly, then snapped her fingers. "Forget burying, they don't deserve such decent treatment. Let's dump them in the moat."

"Brilliant." He grinned. Without further comment, he grabbed William's wrists and dragged him out the door.

"What if the moat dries up?" She said, frowning.

"Doubt it will, remember how much it rains here...but I have an idea."

Knowing her movements would be encumbered by the cloak, she undid it and laid it to the side. Struggling, Briana still managed to drag the smaller redheaded vampire to the doorway by the time Raynor returned. He took over and pulled the body quickly away, while she tugged the blonde vampire to the door, pausing as he reappeared. Catching her breath, she waited for him to return from dumping the larger female, and then followed when he dragged the last male vampire to the edge of the deep ditch.

Raynor picked up a small rock nearby and bent over William' s still form. She watched in puzzlement as he placed it against one fang, reality sinking in as he struck the rock with another larger stone. Reaching inside the open mouth, he withdrew a tiny, pointed tooth, laying it in his palm so she could get a good look. Briana glanced into his eyes and smiled. "That was a great idea."

He nodded distractingly and went back to the task at hand. Each vampire tooth was knocked from each of the shifters and stuck into a pocket of his tunic.

"Wait," she shouted, when he got ready to roll William' s body into the moat. Bending down, she untied the money bag from his waist. Throwing it in the air, she was satisfied with the weighty metal clinks it gave off when it landed on her palm.

"Robbing the dead?"

She frowned at his ill-placed humor. "More like collecting insurance premiums."

Raynor was clearly puzzled by her statement and actions, but stood aside when she removed the coin pouches from each shifter. She laid the bags to the side; then bent down next to him, placing her hands on William' s body.

Shrugging, he repositioned himself and they shoved at the same time, a grim smile of satisfaction lit both their faces when the body bounced and then hit the thick sludge. There was no way to tell how much mire and muck was actually in the stinking mess at the moat's bottom, but when the corpse began to sink slowly, it appeared there was enough to provide an adequate cover for a body.

The other three were pushed off the edge at different areas, but sank into the slime just as efficiently as the leader's body. Briana stood and dusted her hands, and then turned to her companion.

"What about the two young people?"

"We can bury them out in the courtyard. I saw a few holes which will make decent graves." He paused, seemed to wait for her to speak. "What did you have in mind for Robert?"

Without looking at him, she said softly, "He's going home, of course." She picked up the money bags. "These will not be compensation for his loss, but he came looking for treasure, and he's going to return home with some." Tears slipped slowly down her cheeks when she finally faced him.

"It's a thoughtful idea," he said softly.

The pain of his part in the "treasure hunt" came back into his eyes, and she knew it would be a long time before that haunted look left his face.

It took much longer to take care of the young girl and boy. Out of respect, they re-dressed them in the clothes they found pitched unceremoniously in a pile near the wall. Raynor picked up the boy under the arms and she lifted him beneath the knees. She knew he could have easily carried the boy outside himself, but seemed to sense she needed to take part in this portion of the burial.

Fortunately, he'd found two deep holes close to each other. She had the feeling the two young people had been friends, perhaps more. They deserved to spend eternity next to someone who cared for them in life.

The boy's body fit perfectly into the hole. After they brought the girl, it was apparent the hole was slightly short on length. Raynor jumped into the makeshift grave and pitched up rocks while he dug it out with his bare hands. Next, she carefully lowered the girl down; she fit just right now. This thought restarted the tears again. The girl deserved to be alive, enjoying her youth and what life had in store for her. Not a horrible, painful death, and the decay that would follow.

They pushed loose dirt on top of each youth, and then carefully piled rocks on top of the earth. Quickly, Raynor knelt and within a very deep hole, he pitched the vampire teeth. She helped him dump rocks on top.

"What if someone finds them one day?" she asked.

"They will think they're teeth from some animal."

Afterward, they stood in silence, lost in their own thoughts. Briana said a prayer for each of the youths, and then turned back toward the tower, her steps even slower than when she had helped Raynor carry the dead bodies.

The small, pale body lay listlessly on the tabletop, so unlike the vibrant child he'd been that Briana burst into tears again. Raynor took her in his arms and caressed her back, until she stepped back. It took her a few minutes to gain control of herself, but finally she walked to the table, brushed his soft hair from his face and closed his eyes. She straightened his tunic. At least he had not been undressed by the vampires.

She wished she had the strength to carry him all the way to the village, but knew logically she wouldn't be up to the feat. She stepped aside and allowed Raynor to lift the child into his brawny arms.

He turned to her after they exited the tower. "You know, once we take Robert home, people may come to investigate."

"You' re right." She stared at the ruins, hating them with such depth of emotion; it was as if they were a living entity instead of mere stone. "I can' t come back here myself."

Shaking his head in agreement, he said, "I thought as much." He gently laid the young boy on the lush grassy spot where they' d rested. "Why don' t I gather our things and we can get out of here?"

"Do you want me to help?"

"No, stay here with him."

Chapter Sixteen

She knew he was being kind, that her form and voice were so forlorn she wouldn' t be much help anyway. Kneeling beside Robert, she stared into space, her mind a blank slate for a short spell.

Hence she was surprised when Raynor appeared beside her; it seemed but minutes, but by the size of the bundle in his arms, it had to have been more. Smelling smoke, she turned and stared with shock at the towers. Both had thick, black fumes rising from the tiny windows, doorways, and any place a stone had fallen and left a gaping hole in the edifice.

Glancing up at him, she noted the tight shoulders and grim frown.

"I wanted no evidence left of them."

Nodding, she turned back to watch the roiling smoke.

He squatted next to her. "We' d better be going, in case someone comes to investigate the fire."

* * * * *

That was the longest mile she ever walked, taking Robert home to his father — his last journey anywhere. The people came running immediately when they saw the tall Raynor carrying the flopping form of the child. It was late afternoon and most of the villagers were inside their cottages, a few sitting outside. Robert' s father heard the commotion and came running toward them.

They told their made-up story of finding his body near the old ruins and that someone, probably the murderer, had set fire to the towers to cover their tracks. It helped the people to believe them when they handed over the coin filled bags to the father, adding the tale of his son looking for buried treasure and finding it. Whispers began making the rounds and Briana was glad for peoples' lively imaginations. Some thought the poor lad had run across a robber' s nest and found his stash, hence was killed when the robber returned unexpectedly.

She heard no mention of she and Raynor living temporarily in the tower, so Robert must not have shared the information with anyone. Again she was so glad for the child' s help and friendship. Tears dripped down her face, and several villagers patted her kindly. No threat of suspicion surrounded them.

John nodded to them both, his eyes brimming with unshed tears when he took his child from Raynor and turned toward his cottage.

They left soon afterward. She felt bereft somehow, and once again that sense of being lost enveloped her. Walking only a short distance, Raynor took off down a winding trail through a nearby forest. It was already dusky dark under the thick foliage and Briana shivered, imagining all kinds of scary beasts. But then she laughed silently at herself. She' d already met and defeated probably the worst monsters they could run across in this world. Grimly, she thought, *unless you count yourself.*

Soon, they ran across the bubbling stream, the same one that had wound behind the castle. Raynor knelt and refilled their water flask, seeming to be lost in thought or trying to distract himself with busy work. He gathered a large pile of firewood and quickly started a cheery fire. It didn' t help, except to warm her body. Her spirit was as listless as a cold noodle.

Continuing with his activities, he unwrapped the large bundle and began making beds for them. He made a mattress of sorts from fallen leaves, placing the woolen blankets on top. He grunted and waved toward the completed beds. At any other time, she would have found his grunt irritating, but she knew he just didn' t feel like talking, and she didn' t blame him.

The outdoorsy beds were jammed next to each other, and he' d spread the heavy fur on top of both. Hopefully, they' d stay warm through the chilly night with the hot fire and coverings. And, if they were lucky, there' d be no rain.

Exhaustion must have overcome her, for she finally fell into a restless sleep, awaking the next morn groggy and out of sorts. Raynor didn' t look much better; dark circles were under his eyes, making him look like he' d been punched in both very hard. Perhaps he had during the fight yesterday, but Briana had an idea it was sorrow darkening his skin, not blows.

A nondescript breakfast followed, one she washed down with unthinking sips from the flask.

"Stayed pretty warm last night?" he asked her politely, breaking the stillness.

"Yes, but I' ve never been fond of camping." Guilt washed through her once that remark slipped out. Raynor was doing the best he could for them at this point. His next words soothed her conscience, as perhaps he meant them to.

"Me neither." He stared into the woods, where the trees were even denser and sunlight barely penetrated. "I thought I' d try to find a hunter' s cottage Robert told me about earlier." He paused. "I' m sorry, I shouldn' t have—"

She interrupted, "We can' t go around never saying his name again." Looking at him, she tried to put an interested expression on her face. "What did he tell you?"

"Said there was a cottage deeper in the woods, and that no villagers ever go near it."

"Why?"

Clearing his throat, he answered, "It belonged to William."

"And we have no other choice but to use something he owned?" Anger laced her question.

He shrugged. "We need to steer clear of humans, and William' s reputation seems to keep them away." His eyes took in the circumference of the makeshift camp. "This doesn' t provide much shelter, and if any humans happen upon us when we shift..."

His unspoken words told loudly enough of their need to find a safe haven.

"Go on, then, I' ll be fine here. I may take a walk later myself."

Raynor searched her face, as if seeking clues to her true thoughts, but turned away and prepared his side pack. "I' ll be back before nightfall, whether I find it or not."

She nodded, distracted by her own thoughts.

* * * * *

It took him most of the day to find the hunter' s cottage, which was perhaps five miles from their present location, but well-hidden in a profusion of low-growing trees. Several times he thought he heard something slithering through fallen leaves, but never caught a glimpse of who caused the sound. Was Briana pacing the woods, perhaps as the snakewoman? He hoped not, because he wasn' t sure what her reaction would be if she accidentally ran across a human in her present state of mind.

The cottage was satisfactory, being sturdy and made of large blocks of stone. Inside, it was one room, as large as the living room had been in his apartment back home. No furniture graced its interior except one ruggedly-made chair, which looked like it' d been left as an afterthought. The floor was earth, with no rushes. Raynor was glad; he wouldn' t have enjoyed pitching filthy straw out the door in armfuls. Plus, it would have been a sad reminder of the tower.

Thankfully, a nice-sized fireplace took up much of one wall. It looked big enough to roast a pig in, and perhaps it' d been made for just such duty. On the hearth, he discovered a dented bowl, which could be put to many uses, and a large spit hung over the fireplace. He was thrilled with that find. They could stick rabbits and other venison on the rod. There was even a crank to turn the spit, which would make cooking in these primitive conditions much easier.

Placing his pack on the hearth, he kept only the water flask, securing it to his belt. The trip back was much quicker. He set a straight course to the west, following the setting sun, and marked his trail by breaking branches along the way.

Briana was not in camp when he returned and this disturbed him. Was she wandering the woods in such deep sorrow she didn' t pay attention to where she went? Was she lost? In trouble?

On the verge of jumping up and looking for her footprints, he heard a soft rustling in the leaves nearby, and a few minutes later, she appeared. Her form was human, but something told him she had definitely wandered the forest in her snakewoman body. She was upset and could not control her shifting yet, so she' d probably changed without any thought as to the possible consequences.

"Did you find it?"

He nodded. "A nice place too, perfect for our needs."

"Yes, perfect, just like this world," she mumbled.

"We' ll go there tomorrow."

"Fine." She caught his eyes with an intense look. "When do we leave this time period?"

"Remember what I told you about bonding."

Nodding, she said firmly, "Then let' s get started. The sooner we leave this place, the better."

"Don' t you want to eat first?"

"No."

For once, he wished she' d waited a bit—she was acting out of sorrow and anger. Not the best conditions for bonding. Frankly he wasn' t in the mood. He was tired, and his thoughts kept switching back to that small body and his part in the killing of poor little Robert. Then there was the danger of their exposure in such an open area.

But Briana wouldn' t take no for an answer, he could see that in her rigid carriage and set features. Making her point very explicitly, she came over and sat down in his lap. Working with the material and shifting her body from side to side, she positioned her crotch over him. Lord help him, he got hard immediately when he touched her smooth bottom. He' d forgotten ladies didn' t wear underclothes here — one thing he could say he liked about this century.

Her hand reached underneath the bulky cloth covering their bodies and she fiddled with his leggings, grasping his cock. Next, she slid down onto him, encasing him in her warmth in one downward thrust.

In spite of his misgivings, he was aroused by her wet heat. Suddenly, he did want to make love to this beautiful, tortured woman. The next minute, she shifted and it was the snake goddess who rode him like a fiend. Their session didn' t last long; she was too wild, too intent on gaining a momentary pleasure. She drove him over the brink in a few minutes with her wiggling body and inside massage that felt like a frenzied dance. Like a horde of tiny Leprechauns were doing the Riverdance on his cock; at least that was the crazy image his imagination dredged up.

After their lovemaking, Briana reappeared and he wished it' d been her he' d had sex with. The snakewoman was wildly satisfying, but he had a deep longing to fully experience the human side of Briana, her needs, and to know her body as well as the shifter side.

* * * * *

Their life fell into a pattern after they settled into the cottage. Briana went on frequent walks or sat and stared into space. She was too caught up in her inner world; she seemed to have completely forgotten about their need to bond. He hunted, fished, and brought in firewood, while she cooked the food. No further lovemaking fell into that routine, since she didn' t initiate any and he didn' t feel as if he should push her.

After a few days, Raynor lay awake a long time, thinking about Briana. He hadn' t known much about her when he was dream calling—she was too far away for a proper connection. Besides, her unknowing state about her shifter heritage caused a big rift in the link they should have established through the years before they met.

But he had discovered much about her since jumping to this time period. She was strong in both body and spirit, taking on everything that had been thrown at her with a sense of humor. Her tenderness toward Robert proved her kindhearted and interested in children. She was intelligent, resourceful, thoughtful, and sweet. A virtual Girl Scout. Raynor grinned at his own silliness.

In reality, she was everything he' d ever hoped for when thinking of the perfect match for himself. Her beauty and sexual charisma were outstanding and he couldn' t think of any other qualities he would add to that list. Even her snakewoman was sizzling, heroic, and exciting.

His beautiful princess had been temporarily ousted by a sad, grieving woman. He hoped she worked through her pain soon; otherwise they might be stuck here for quite a while. The medieval experience wasn' t so bad, but he was ready to go home. Ready to start his new life with his lovely Briana. They had been mated by the psychic link of their people, but he' d also fallen deeply, irrevocably in love with this wonderful woman.

Finally, after a week of her grief, he thought it was time to move on, that they must work on their bonding. He returned with a fresh catch of trout and found her sitting on the one chair, staring into the fire. He' d already cleaned the catch outside, and it took only a few minutes to prepare them for the spit. Afterwards, he knelt down in front of her and took her hands in his.

"Briana, aren' t you ready to go home?"

Chapter Seventeen

Coming out of her self-induced haze, her eyes stared into his with clarity. "Yes, I want to go home."

"Then, sweetheart, we have to start working on bonding."

Briana physically threw herself backwards, almost tipping over in the chair. "I can' t. It seems disrespectful to be enjoying myself when he' s lying in a cold grave."

Raynor understood perfectly. When he' d lost his beloved grandfather, everything he did that brought him pleasure—fishing, going to movies, dining out, and making love—seemed wrong somehow. The very act of living and being alive in a vibrant way, while his grandfather rotted in a cemetery, didn' t seem right.

Grasping her hands again, he said softly, "We don' t have to make love, there' s other steps to bonding that are just as important, and frankly should be worked through before engaging in sex."

Her jaw clenched when she said, "Then why have we been going at each other like dogs?"

"It' s the natural attraction we feel, can' t be helped at first."

"So, now what?" She frowned.

"I start training you how to stay in human form and how to become as one with me."

"That second part sounds very…weird."

"It' s not as bad as it sounds." His chuckle drew a slight smile from her.

"Do you feel up to starting now?" At her nod, he jumped up and brought the fur throw from where it lay on their makeshift beds. Then he placed it in front of the fireplace and put a large log on the fire. The room brightened and warmed to a pleasant temperature.

Settling on the fur, he sat cross-legged and looked up at her. Patting the place in front of him, he waited until she sat down facing him. It took a few seconds, but she finally got the skirt of the dress to cooperate so she could sit as he did. "Now, just close your eyes and breathe."

"What?"

"Just do it."

She did, but a few moments later, cracked her eyes and peered at his relaxed features. "Are we meditating?"

His eyelids opened half way and his peaceful golden gaze locked with hers. "Yes," he whispered.

Getting the hint, Briana closed her eyes and tried to concentrate on breathing. It wasn' t as easy as she would have thought. Somehow, thinking about her breathing seemed to make her so conscious of it, she took erratic breaths. And her mind, she couldn' t stop its ruminating. Robert' s sweet memory was etched into almost every corner.

Still, Raynor didn' t say a word, and she knew he could probably hear her off-beat breathing. Heck, she wouldn' t doubt he was aware of her very thoughts either. He seemed to have uncanny abilities when it came to her. Since he didn' t stop to tell her she wasn' t doing it right, she kept on. After what seemed like an eternity, her body relaxed and Briana's mind wandered in places other than those captured by sorrow.

An interminable time later, she heard a distant growling noise, opened her eyes, and giggled. She couldn't help it. Raynor's stomach was protesting loudly. Sighing, he slid his eyes open slowly and grinned.

"Guess we'd better eat."

"You're not the only hungry one." She smiled.

They prepared dinner together, which wasn't hard since the fish he'd put on the spit earlier had cooked to a mouthwatering tenderness. Briana scraped and chopped a few raw vegetables, and they added a slice of fresh bread he'd bought yesterday.

The evening was pleasant, sitting in front of the fire, sipping homemade mint tea. They chatted amiably about nothing in particular. Raynor seemed intent on not bringing up any subject which could be construed as painful. While she appreciated this thoughtfulness, it began to make her feel silly also, like she was some fragile female who couldn't stand up to the challenges life threw her.

Nodding dreamily to herself, Briana realized that this is just how she'd been acting, that it was time to come out of her pain-filled stupor and face the world. If she wanted to return to good ol' twenty-first century America, that was exactly what she had to do.

Sleep that night was much more restful than it had been all week. She lay awake for some time though, thinking about their meditation session early that day, and wondering what tomorrow would bring.

The next day they spent a few hours practicing breathing and "centering". Briana had to admit she was much better at breathing slow and relaxing on the second try. Raynor was pleased with her progress.

They took a long leisurely stroll in the woods afterwards; nature seemed to calm her even more, and she felt better than she had in a while. Talk revolved around their lives back home and they found they had many things in common. They both loved exercise, especially hiking in the woods. They enjoyed action movies and relished human holidays and all the festivities. Many more topics were discussed and they were amazed at the connections between them concerning their views on life.

After arriving back at the cottage, Raynor dragged out the make-shift checker board and pieces he' d created one evening. She had stared in curiosity when he unfurled a large square section of dried leather he' d brought back from his latest trip to the village. He' d spent hours carefully painting crude squares with a mixture of wild berries, using his finger like a brush. Then he' d dabbed berry juice on twelve acorns; hence designating them the red checkers, while the unpainted ones were the black ones.

Admittedly she hadn' t been sure exactly what he was doing until he' d waved her to sit across from him and play a game. Crude or not the board and acorn pieces worked quite well. Of course crowning the King turned into a gigglefest. Raynor had placed a pile of acorn ends nearby and each time one of them exclaimed "King me", they had to try and fit the cap onto the wild nut. Sometimes it fit tightly and sometimes the end tumbled off during the game. They' d quickly fallen into a routine of playing several nightly games of checkers, in spite of the poor quality of the parts.

Later that evening, after their checker game, while they sat sipping their tea in front of the fire, her mind went back to questions she had concerning the Reeshon. She'd forgotten them until now, but her relaxed state seemed to bring them to mind again.

"Raynor, remember when I asked before about the bad shifters?" At his nod, she continued, "I was wondering if anyone does anything to punish such evil creatures?"

"As a matter of fact, we have terminator shapeshifters who kill them, exterminate them so to speak."

"But, wouldn't knowing about the terminators stop them from slaughtering people?'

"Maybe it would stop some, if they knew. It's a big secret."

"Wait a minute, then how do you know about it?" Her eyes opened wide. "Are you a terminator?"

He shook his head. "No, although I've thought about it. I have a good friend who is, and he shared the secret with me." He smiled at her. "With a threat to never tell anyone, of course."

"Then why tell me?"

He reached out and gently held her hands. "Because I think it's very important for you to know. Just don't tell anyone else, or I might have to kill you."

Smiling, she turned serious again the next instant. "But why not let shifters know about this killing squad?"

"It'd make it harder and more dangerous for the terminators to find the perpetrators. Of course, evil bastards, such as those vampires, or insane shifters wouldn't be scared off from their prey anyway."

She nodded in understanding, and then looked at him intensely. "You have crazy shifters?"

"Sure, just like humans, only they' re much worse. Thankfully, they are also rare." He gave her hands a squeeze. "Remember Jack the Ripper?"

She snorted at his question. "Who doesn' t?" Her eyes shot to his. "Don' t tell me he was a shifter?"

Raynor nodded. "Went insane, got stuck in between, wasn' t totally human or a shifter when the urge to kill struck him."

"What was he?" she whispered.

"Werewolf in his true form, but something in between when he tried to shift."

Shivering, she asked, "Did the terminators take him out?"

"You got it."

"Good." She stared into space, trying to imagine the horror those poor women faced before being ripped apart. "What about the women he killed?"

"No time ripple; therefore, they were fated to die. Victorian England was hard on humans, especially prostitutes. Disease, alcohol, hard living." He paused. "Although, there were two other women the cleaners went back and saved from being murdered—they weren' t slated for death."

"Really? The terminators can save people before the fact?"

"Not the terminators. We have shifters who ' clean up' mistakes made by shapeshifters, whether it' s preventing someone from being killed, or cleaning up dumb mistakes, like teaching humans how to do something before its time in history."

"Like how to pole-fish if it' s not the proper time?"

"Yes." He frowned. "But a better example would be teaching a man how to start a fire using a modern method."

"Cleaners, now that sounds like an interesting idea." They were quiet for a few minutes, and then she asked, "Do you think the elders would have sent terminators after the vampires?"

He nodded, "I suspect so. I have a feeling those young people weren' t the first humans they' d killed."

"What about Robert? Do you think it might not have been his time to die?"

Staring at her, he said, "Maybe not."

"Does that mean the elders might send cleaners back?" she asked.

"Yes, if they pick up a ripple surrounding his death."

Hugging her body to hold in a shiver that hit her, Briana mumbled, "Please, please, let it be a mistake."

* * * * *

The next day, Raynor changed tactics, telling her to hold his hands while they meditated. She found this to be a pleasant experience, except for the tingles that shot from his hands to hers. Shoving erotic thoughts from her mind was difficult, but she had to in order to maintain the peaceful nature of their meditation.

For several days following the holding of hands, Raynor instructed her to concentrate on his being, meaning his breathing and heartbeat. She was to synchronize her body rhythms with his. It seemed an impossible order, but she tried, getting very frustrated the first day. But, by the end of the third day, it was as if his heartbeat was her own and his breath flowed into her, even though they were two different beings.

When this connection happened, it was sudden, and her whole body vibrated with little sharp tickles, as if tiny hands were running up and down on the inside of her nerves. "Oh," she breathed out in a slight sigh.

"Open your eyes," he ordered gently.

She did, astounded by the colors surrounding his body, and glancing down, saw the soft red, blue, purple, and yellow, also flowed gently around her. His stare pulled at her like a physical action, and when she locked with his golden orbs, it did become a physical reaction. It was a scary, disorientating sensation — like she was pulled outside her body and into his. Her mind was crawling around the fringes of his; she could see herself through his eyes, feel how soft her skin was when he touched her.

It was too much, this spiraling, out of control feeling of being blended with another person. Briana physically jerked her body backwards and the contact broke.

Chapter Eighteen

"I' m sorry."

He smoothed the hair at her brow. "Don' t worry, you did wonderful. When we can maintain the contact, then we' ll be bonded."

"I' m frightened. This…thing, it' s beyond anything I' ve ever known."

"Of course it is. You told me your parents died when you were ten, so you never had anyone explain or teach your heritage to you."

Anger shot through her when he mentioned her parents. She loved them dearly, but wished they had told her of her people. Right then, though, she couldn' t think about them, she had to keep a clear head and listen to Raynor' s words. Changing the subject, she asked, "Why are we ' mated' ?"

"Mating is difficult to understand…it' s rather mysterious. Two shapeshifters are linked psychically. No one, not even the elders understand how this process works. But, when a shifter begins to sense his mate' s essence, the male sends a call to her in her dreams."

"Do the women feel the men as well?"

He shook his head no. "Not until the male begins to send to her."

"What if a male doesn' t find his mate?"

"It has happened…it is a sad thing." He pointed a finger to his chest. "I'm fifty years old, so I was without a shifter mate for a long time until I sensed your presence."

"Fifty!"

"Remember, we live to around two hundred, so I'm still in my prime."

Briana blushed. "I didn't mean." She halted her lame statement; saying it made it sound worse. Instead, she asked, "What if I hadn't come along?"

He shrugged. "If a mate is never found, a shifter can choose a human partner, or they can choose to jump." His expression was rock serious and she got the impression he wouldn't have liked to consider such an alternative.

"Does that work, between a shifter and human?"

"It has, although a shifter always prefers a Reeshon mate whenever possible. If they marry a human, they must be very careful to never shift in front of them."

"Even if the human is trustworthy?"

"The danger is too great. Such acts are highly discouraged."

"What did you mean by a shifter jumping if they find no mate?"

"That the shifter can choose a century they really like and jump in the hope they can find a mate there. But, if they don't, they can't return."

"How sad." To think, a shifter might live several hundred years and never find their true mate. It was too horrible to contemplate. Now as she looked back, she understood her deep loneliness through the years and dissatisfaction with every human male she'd dated.

"Of course, even if they find a shifter, say in the Medieval era, they can' t jump back to the future with their mate anyway." At her curious look, he continued, "You can only jump into the past. A mate from the past has not been born, so she or he couldn' t jump forward."

"But they could jump into the past together?"

"No," he shook his head. "The shifter from the future would be ' known' by the elders from his or her time frame. His essence would be unrecognizable to the elders of the past." Noticing her confusion, he explained, "When we bond to gain the elders' attention, it' s like we' re dialing up a phone number. If the elders recognize the caller, then they answer."

"Caller ID!" She laughed.

"You could *call* it that." His wry grin was hard to resist, but she wanted to understand, so chose to ignore his silly pun.

"But how does this recognition work?"

"Shifters bring their children to meet the elders; they imprint on them, so they can be recognized."

"But I wasn' t brought to the elders?"

"No." He smiled at her happily. "Luckily for you and me, the elders were able to pick up your essence from your presence in the cave; they drew it in immediately and it imprinted on them."

"This is pretty hard information to absorb." She knit her brow in thought. "So," she mused, "if a shifter jumps into the past to look for a mate, they better be darn sure they wouldn' t mind living out their life in that time." Staring into the fire, she said, "But what if they found a shifter from the future, who had jumped looking for a mate as well?"

"Then, they could jump back into the twenty-first century if they wished."

Giving him a slight smile, she said, "I've got a lot to learn."

"And you can, once we jump back. Of course, you'll be in a classroom with shifter children."

"Thanks," she said with a wry humor. "Just what I want, to go back to school."

They spent the rest of the evening getting to know each other better. Raynor shared details about his job, friends, and hobbies. Phoenix was his hometown and she loved hearing about its highpoints, while he enjoyed her stories of living in a big southern city. Now she understood why she'd perceived his call as very distant— they lived so far apart, and why she heard him clearer when she came on vacation.

Later, in bed, Briana thought about their conversations that day and realized several important facts. She really liked Raynor. They seemed to have many things in common, more than she had shared with Mark. Even their views on politics, the environment, and child-rearing were similar. It seemed like she'd known him for years; his newfound friendship was comfortable.

The mating call could be responsible for that she guessed. He'd been "talking" to her in her dreams for years. But then again, maybe it was a mixture of dream calling and the psychic mating. She didn't know exactly what it was, but Raynor seemed more suited to her needs and desires as a potential husband then anyone she'd ever dated. In the physical realm, he had no equal in looks in her eyes. And his sexual experience was superior, while the sizzle between them was explosive. Maybe, she wondered to herself, her feelings could be summed up as love? But since she' d never been in love before, she just wasn' t sure.

* * * * *

The next day, he suggested they try making love while tuning in to each other and see if they could maintain the special bonding during the excitement phase.

Raynor was a tender lover, stroking her body with circular caresses that drove her crazy with their erotic intensity. His calloused hands grazing down her sensitive flesh evoked quivers of anticipation. He didn' t concentrate just on her breasts, as some of her lovers in the past had done, but gave every inch of her skin attention.

Long strokes passed down her side, over her hips and down her legs. A massage to her feet relaxed her even further, and then his caresses slowly traveled up her legs, gently circling her upper thighs, until she thought the fur throw would be soaked with her response. Each time her excitement reached a fevered pitch, he would pause and gaze hypnotically into her eyes, reconnecting with her.

Next, his hands were replaced with his warm, wet tongue, laving her flesh from neck to belly button in a snail pace that made her want to grab his hair and shove him to the place that ached for his attention. When his head finally traveled down to her curls and his tongue dipped several times into her lips, flicking her clit into a wet, aching maelstrom, she discerned the snakewoman emerging. She could almost smell her excitement, and groaned in frustration. Briana tried mightily to reconnect with Raynor, to no avail. Her limbs trembled violently while she slipped into a fugue state. Their session ended in a wild frenzy, as usual once that creature appeared.

* * * * *

"I' m sorry," she said later, when she lay snuggled in his arms.

Kissing the top of her head, Raynor said, "You did very well, actually. It takes time."

"How much time?"

"You' re asking me something I don' t know, my love. I' ve never had a shifter mate before."

Turning to peer up at him, she smiled into his handsome face. "I' m glad."

The rest of the day they spent exploring the woods around the cottage, something they both enjoyed immensely.

Later, Raynor grabbed his homemade fishing pole and they tried their luck in the stream. Briana had never fished before and found it more fun than she would have guessed, except for putting the bait on. Her partner laughingly slid the fat grubs they' d dug from beneath a log, onto the hook with teasing protests.

* * * * *

The following day, they were ready to try making love again. This time though, Raynor suggested they meditate first, which they did. By the time they got ready to try, she was fully relaxed. They faced each other across the fur throw while a bright fire kept them warm.

Raynor' s hands stroked up one arm, all the way up to her face. She knew without opening her eyes that his were still closed, that he caressed her by touch only. She also knew he wanted her to follow his lead, which she did, letting her hands find the planes of his face. Exploring gently, she memorized its features with her fingertips. When she reached his lips, she lingered over his lower lip.

The next instant he sucked in softly, drawing one finger into his warm, wet mouth. She shivered. The experience was delicious, sinful. While he worked on her finger, his hand came up and stroked her lips. Reciprocating, she drew his wandering forefinger into her mouth. She both felt his responding shiver and sensed it in her own body. They were connecting again, except this time the sensations were far more intense.

Briana lost track of time, but it seemed they explored each other' s bodies, fully-clothed, for hours. She knew the texture of his ridged muscles beneath the wool, the curliness of his leg hairs underneath his hose, and the rock-hard cock which met her curious hand when she rubbed the tunic that covered it.

Raynor had tracked his hands over her whole body as well, touching her curves beneath the silk. By the time he gently turned her so he could unlace the dress, she was breathing heavy, as was he. They made the ritual of undressing as slow and erotic as the mutual exploration of each other' s bodies. Raynor' s hands grazed her flesh in every part that was exposed, as he slid the sleeves down her arms. Following his lead, she did the same as she helped him with the tunic. Adding her own playfulness, she smoothed her hands in gentle strokes over his hard chest and tweaked each nipple. The muscles that tightened in his abs told her the caresses were turning him on.

She stood briefly so he could slide the dress down. This time he kissed each piece of skin that was exposed by the fabric' s earthward journey. Her nipples had pebbled and her pussy had become quite wet by the time he finished.

She knelt as he stood and helped him off with his leggings. His staff kept nudging her head as she worked the hose. Rubbing one cheek, then her lips against his cock's silken strength, she was gratified with the groan that escaped him.

"Briana." His words caught, and he rubbed his hand through her hair.

Moving down his muscular thighs, she placed kisses and tiny nibbles along his skin as she uncovered it. His breathing was heavy.

When completely nude, Briana stretched on the fur throw, rubbing her whole body back and forth, pushing into the luxurious pile. Their eyes were opened by now and she saw Raynor's golden eyes latch onto her thrusting breasts when her back arched. For once, shyness stayed at bay and she gave him back a bold look, going over his magnificent body with eyes as hot as his own.

"You're so beautiful," he whispered softly, running one hand down her side.

"And you." His grin told her he didn't think men were beautiful, but he didn't refute her statement.

Raynor leaned over her, gave her tiny kisses all over her face, finally settling on her mouth. By this time she was aching to suckle his lips and tongue. They were so delicious, these shifter kisses and the instruments that delivered them.

His free hand came into play, caressing her body up and down, while she ran hers along his muscular torso. She was overcome with excitement so deep she could barely stand it. She wanted him inside her right this minute, pounding her brains out, but at the same time, she wanted this special time to last. So, instead, she concentrated on the kissing and tried to ignore her erotically pumping senses. She groaned into his mouth and soft sighs of "oh" escaped her every few seconds.

When he moved to her breasts, she trembled in reaction and pushed his head down into her soft flesh. Suddenly, she wanted even more intensity. In response, Raynor squeezed her tender flesh with firmer strokes, and his tongue and teeth applied more pressure. Arching her back, she encouraged this hard assault.

When he moved down her body, he stopped just above her mons and looked up at her. "Do I dare?"

"Yes," she answered breathlessly. She still had control, still felt as one with him.

His face dipped into her cleft, his tongue following, and Briana did think for a few seconds she was going to lose control of her human side. But biting her lower lip while her lower body went mad with sensation, she was determined to hold on this time. His tongue was so soft, so wet and warm. It was a deliciously sinful feeling. Her clit throbbed, but as yet, he slipped around it, wetting her folds and even dipping his tongue into her vagina. He was driving her crazy.

"Mmm, your tongue feels so good," she panted.

Swirling, long strokes, licks, and sucking motions erupted from his tongue and lips, centered this time on her clit. She ground her head against the soft fur in reaction. Her legs trembled and her belly clenched. Abruptly, a huge orgasm gripped her and Raynor held onto her hips while she bucked wildly, riding it out for long seconds of endless, ecstatic pleasure. Briana screamed at the peak, and then flopped weakly onto the fur throw, her body totally spent.

"What did you do to me?" she asked in a panting voice.

Raynor positioned himself above her, leaned down and placed a tender kiss to her lips. "Gave you pleasure...human pleasure."

She watched while he settled between her thighs, his cock poised at her entrance. Then he barely pushed it inside, withdrew, and repeated this action for at least a full minute. She wouldn' t have believed such a small movement could drive her up the wall, but it did. He was teasing her and she was loving it.

Firmly, he shoved into her with one long stroke and she moaned aloud at the swift switch in tactic. She ran her hands through his hair and tightened her grip against his scalp. He descended, catching her in a steamy kiss and she latched onto his lips as if for sustenance. And he was food for her...she needed him right now, more than she' d ever craved food.

He filled her with his large cock, her body with his shifter essence, and her mind with the bonding that connected them. Glimmers of his feelings shot through her own sensual haze at times, causing their lovemaking to be confusing sometimes, but nothing short of mind-blowing in eroticism. His hardness pumped into her, and her own wet softness invaded her senses, as if she were in Raynor' s mind. She felt the downy delicateness of her flesh when he stroked it, while her own hands stroked the ridged muscles of his frame.

It was too much and it was not enough at the same time. Her whole body clenched when her vagina gripped his staff with her second big climax. She frantically sucked on his tongue, seeking to draw every drop of sensation she could from contact with him. When her orgasm ripped through her body, colors swirled in her mind, danced through her brain cells and along her nerve endings at the same time. Her breath merged with Raynor's and his orgasm became her own. She screamed loudly when her mate threw back his head and let loose with a manly bellow of his own.

* * * * *

Afterwards, Raynor cuddled her in his arms. "We did it," she said softly.

Kissing the top of her head, he said. "Yes, we did."

"When can we go back home?"

"Anytime you wish."

Briana sighed happily. "Just not today." She covered a yawn.

"How about tomorrow?"

"Sounds perfect." Her voice petered out as she drifted off to sleep.

Chapter Nineteen

"Are you ready to jump?"

"As ready as I' ll ever be," she answered nervously.

It had taken more than a few minutes to locate the large boulder Briana had sat on after she first walked through the portal. But it took less time to find the area between the two large oaks, where the portal opening was situated.

"Hold my hand." He stuck out his and she grasped it firmly, sweating nervously. "Remember what I taught you."

She closed her eyes and concentrated on Raynor' s essence: his heartbeat, breathing, and the chemical connection she perceived with every particle of her being. Their breathing and heart rate synchronized until she was aware of the barest brush of his thoughts against her mind.

Time ticked by, no way to know how much. Suddenly, a strong electric current ripped through her and leapt across to her mate. The next instant, she was jolted with an exchange of electricity from Raynor' s hand. Cracking her eyes, Briana held her breath. The archway had appeared.

The cave interior was in front of them and three old people stood near the portal. Their expressions were kind and welcoming.

With a tug, Raynor led her to the arch and they stepped through. She was shocked; it was so simple. But then, it' d been all that preparatory work that was hard.

"Welcome back, my children," the oldest looking male said.

"This is Bhaskar," her mate introduced him, and then the other two. Respect was prominent in his tone and attitude.

"Did you have any problems?" Gorna asked.

Raynor nodded, his eyes serious.

"Will you excuse us for a short while?" Bhaskar waved an arm at a nearby couch.

Curiosity riveted her, but she realized they wanted Raynor to themselves. Some kind of report she guessed. The four shifters disappeared through a doorway. Would he tell them about her? About the snakewoman?

After five minutes, Briana was too restless; she wanted to see what was going on. Treading softly, she peeked inside the open door; it was small and cozy. All four sat on the floor, holding hands. It reminded her of a séance. Sensing she'd intruded on something ceremonial, she withdrew and sat for another five minutes. Would they never finish? What were they discussing? What did they think of her? She was becoming more nervous as the minutes ticked by.

Her handsome lover joined her on the couch at last, while the three elders sat down in heavily padded chairs across from them.

"Why don't you share your shifter being?" Chao asked unexpectedly.

Not her, she thought and gave them an uncomfortable stare.

"Not the snakewoman," Gorna's dark eyes twinkled in understanding. "The one that will call the twenty-first century home."

Although she had not mentioned the snakewoman, somehow, they knew about her. Oh God, they must have discussed her. She would ask Raynor later; it must be that ceremony. Perhaps it was their way of exchanging important information.

"But, I don' t know what I am." She couldn' t keep the tremble from her voice.

"That' s why we asked, my child," Bhaskar said. "We can help, if you have difficulties."

Difficulties, she repeated in her head, too scared to ask them what the heck they meant.

They regarded her with calm, reassuring expressions, but the thought of stripping naked in front of three strangers was too much. A vivid blush burned her cheeks.

The three elders looked at each other, then Bhaskar stood and walked off some distance, while Chao and Gorna took positions by their chairs.

"Shifters feel no shame in their forms, no matter which is manifested, including human," the leader said quietly. "But, we know you were not raised to understand this; therefore, we will make you comfortable with your own kind."

With that emphatic statement, he unzipped the full-length robe, which reminded her of a wizard' s garment, the exotic, beautiful embroidery marking its hem, lending credence to this thought. The robe fell to his feet, and Bhaskar stepped out of the pooled fabric—a thin, nude old man. Briana was shocked by the fact that even though he looked aged even in human years, he was in very good shape. His chest was firm, his limbs slim but muscular. Her eyes averted from his groin area; it seemed disrespectful.

She noticed movement from Chao and Gorna, and when she turned she saw they' d stripped as well. The male elder was stoutly built, but surprisingly well-endowed across his chest and legs. Gorna was slender as a reed, but her figure was shockingly in good shape as well, her breasts barely drooping at all.

Movement in the other direction drew her eyes back to the leader. Bhaskar was surrounded by a mist. Briana sucked in her breath. She was about to be privileged with a rare sight; she sensed this deep inside. She was more curious than a cat who' d discovered a bag with kitty goodies inside. Raynor had told her what shifters the elders transformed into, but she couldn' t remember, and suddenly didn' t want to. She wanted to be delighted.

It took less than a minute for the light show and foggy haze to dissipate. The creature that appeared was legendary and unbelievable. A huge dragon. It was an iridescent red, with huge leathery wings folded neatly along its back. Unthinking, she hugged her body with a protective gesture, but then shame flushed through her when she recognized Bhaskar' s kind eyes shining from the gigantic head. "You' re magnificent," she whispered, hoping to make up for her momentary doubt. The dragon dipped its head and she knew she' d been forgiven.

A flash of light drew her attention back to the others. "Oh," Briana gushed when her eyes landed on a mythical unicorn, so lovely her eyes teared in wonder. White with a hint of blue — just as the stories always told the tale, with a two foot pale blue horn and sky bright eyes to match.

The last shifter was Chao. She had no doubt, for facing her was an awe-inspiring centaur, with Chao' s face and upper body. From his waist down, a majestic black steed pranced — its lower body joining the elder at the horse' s shoulders. He was the most bizarre looking of the three, but still majestic. Now, she could understand why ancient humans both feared and worshiped the rare mystical creatures they spotted.

"Don' t I rate an ' oh' ?" The ever cheerful countenance of Chao drew into a moue of discontent.

"Oh, yes," she said sincerely. "You just overwhelmed me."

He laughed, an odd sound, a mixture of human and horse snorting.

"Thank you, all of you." She turned to each in succession.

The elders dipped their head in acknowledgement, and then looked at her with those wondrous, magical faces and bodies. She knew she could no longer refuse their kind invitation, for she suddenly realized they would help her if she had problems shifting. But, she also knew they extended an honor to her. How she knew this, she didn' t have a clue, but she knew it was fact. To have such prestigious creatures ask to see the true shifter self, was not offered to every shapeshifter that walked into this secret place.

Springing up quickly, Briana let go the last of her qualms, and undressed swiftly until she stood nude. She concentrated on shifting like Raynor had taught her. Pain no longer lanced through her system and the process overtook her as easily as butter melting on a hot stove.

She watched her lover' s face through the mist. When it cleared, he looked as astounded as the day she' d first changed into the snakewoman. What was she?

Glancing down hesitantly, she was shocked too. Her legs were covered in brown hair; no, fur. With her typical wry humor, she thought to herself, she'd never again complain about her leg hairs being too long.

Bringing her hands in front of her face, Briana examined the furry hands, tipped with impressive claws. Next, she brought those hairy hands carefully to her face and touched it all over. Hairy as well. Finally, with a tremble, she turned to Raynor.

"What am I?"

He stepped forward and gripped her hands tightly, a joyful expression on his handsome face. "Same as me, werewolf."

"Ooh," she wasn't sure how she felt about that, but her mate's whole attitude was so happy, glimmers of pleasure began to radiate throughout her body.

"Is that a good thing?"

"The best," he answered and then his gaze became disconnected.

Briana continued to hold Raynor's hands while he slipped into shifting, but she turned to the elders. Without having to ask, they answered her unspoken question.

"It is a wondrous match when mates are the same shapeshifter form," Bhaskar said.

"Why?"

"Fertility is very low among our people," he replied. "We don't know if it's Earth's environment or if our people never had high rates to begin with. That's why there are not large numbers of shapeshifters in existence, and probably why we have been rarely seen by humans."

Bhaskar peered at her with a happy expression, one to match Raynor's. "But, when a mated couple is matched in shifter forms, it increases the chances of them producing offspring."

"Really?" Her tone was not questioning, but happy.

She felt the change in Raynor' s hand without having to see the fog had dissipated. Briana turned and looked fully at her mate for the first time as a female werewolf. And she thought she' d been turned on the first time she saw him shift? Every molecule in her body wanted to leap onto him, savage him with teeth and claws while she plunged onto his cock.

She trembled and saw by Raynor' s expression, he wanted the same thing. He seemed barely in control of himself.

"My children, we will withdraw into the next chamber and take a break." With that emphatic statement the three elders shifted in quicksilver speed and walked briskly down a tunnel.

Briana noticed immediately why they' d shifted before leaving. Bhaskar' s head wouldn' t have fit into the tunnel, much less his huge dragon body.

"Why did they leave?"

"To give us privacy."

Raynor' s voice was deeper than normal, a growling tone underlying it. The new quality of his vocal chords sent shivers down her spine, her reaction issuing from sexual need. His very voice made her horny.

"Privacy?" Her hands stroked down his arms, leaving furrows in his hair.

"They know that mated couples who shift for the first time, in their own time period, have an uncontrollable urge to fuck."

Briana didn' t like that word under normal circumstances, and had never heard him use it either. But, the savage emotions welling up inside her, wanted release in the most primal form possible. Wanted to feel, think, taste, hear, and smell sex in its rawest state.

Surprising her, he grabbed their clothes, and then quickly bounded across the room to stand in the doorway of the small room he and the elders occupied earlier. "It has a door, in case they come back too soon," he said as he held the door open.

Licking her lips in anticipation, Briana sprang past her mate and listened while he slammed shut the heavy door. She didn' t turn, wanted to take in his approach with every sense she had at her disposal. His musky, half-human, half-wolf odor wafted around her body like the sweetest perfume. Thick nails clicked on the stone flooring, and she shivered, as if his nails tracked slowly along her spine instead of the floor.

Hair-covered arms came around her middle from behind, yanking her to him with one forceful jerk. His body was hard, the muscles bulging in all the right places, yet also soft because of the fur. It was a delicious sensation, this twining of firmness and softness. Raking his tongue along her neck, he pulled her ear into his mouth, making her whimper as the wet heat assaulted her sensitive earlobe.

Breaking from his grasp abruptly, she fell to her knees and crawled on all fours to a large sheepskin rug. It was even downier than her or Raynor' s hair. Crouching down, she rubbed her face into the plush fabric, and then from her position, turned her face up and back at him. "Come." Command and yearning was in her voice.

Chapter Twenty

Her mate leapt at her and posed his body over hers. Both hands grabbed her breasts from behind, kneaded and squeezed them with force. She moaned and arched her back. He growled, and then clawed through her fur slightly, so that his talons sleeked down her breasts, teasing, but not cutting into the meat. Claws tweaked her nipples, made them ache to be suckled.

As if sensing her need, he slid off her back and slipped underneath her and Briana shifted her arms to accommodate him beneath her. He played with her breasts from this new position, even slapped them, making them sway tantalizingly in front of his face. Tired of his teasing, she shoved one breast toward his mouth and it opened in a great wolfish grin as he sucked it in with fervor. Greedy, slurping noises emitted from him and moans of wild pleasure from her.

Her lower body was on fire and there was only one way to soothe such a savage beast. "I must have you inside me—now," she panted.

Raynor grabbed her arms and she knew he planned to flip her over.

"No," she pulled against his brawny arms. "This way." She wiggled her hips. "As it should be with our kind."

Springing up quickly once he moved from beneath her, he repositioned himself behind her. "You mean doggie," his voice was rough-edged, barely in control.

"Wolfie, if you like." She laughed deep in her throat, her laughter turning to a tiny howl when he suddenly plunged into her without warning. Pulling back with an agonizingly slow movement that made her squirm, he circled his thrusts, making her lips swell even more.

He was so large; he filled her up. His moves were primordial, untamed, and her body inside became slick in reaction. It hurt slightly, yet it was a pleasurable pain, one she desired more of. "Yes," she whispered, then said louder, "harder, harder," wiggling her hips for encouragement.

Raynor needed no encouragement. But, when she panted those words, his hands gripped her hips harder and his furry hips thudded against her butt in a frenzied, steely rhythm that whipped up throbbing responses in her groin.

"Yes," she screamed, her excitement close to peaking. "Fuck me, my wolf."

Growling, his body plunged over hers and his teeth sank into her shoulder. She arched her hips upward, meeting him thrust for thrust, groaning and wriggling her lower body in faster circles while her excitement built.

Suddenly, she screamed and bucked. Her mate loosened his hold on her shoulder and slammed into her with mighty lunges, his whole body thrown behind his strokes. A howl cut the air when his seed spurted into her with powerful pumps. That howl made her stomach clench. Her vagina tightened around him like a vise and it shuddered inside around his cock. She answered his primitive howl with one of her own, her clit pulsing, and her folds coating them both with slick wetness.

They fell forward onto the rug; rolling to the side, her mate wrapped her in his arms. She was sated and content. Stroking his furry arm, Briana felt her eyelids become heavy. She was startled from the lassitude that gripped her when she felt the shift coming over her again. At her back, Raynor changed as well.

After her human form reappeared, she twisted around, facing him. He smoothed a lock of hair behind her ear, a tender gesture she found endearing. "Will it always be that hot?"

He chuckled. "We will have more…restraint from now on, but yes, it will seem like we' re caught in the middle of a firestorm each time. At least, that' s what I' ve been told."

"Mmm. I can' t say that' s a bad thing." She snuggled beneath his chin. They chatted for a few minutes, calming their sensitive systems down to normal levels.

"I hear the elders coming back."

"Me too." Briana sat up. "We' d better rejoin them?" she asked a little uncertainly, unsure of Reeshon etiquette.

He sighed in an overly exaggerated fashion. "It wouldn' t be polite to keep them waiting now." He sprang up and held out a hand to haul her up. "Besides, it' s time for us to be going."

Briana wanted to ask where they were going, but suddenly she was unclear as to what the future held for them. What if his answer was something she didn' t want to hear?

They redressed quickly. Taking one last look around, she burned the memory of this room into her mind. She never wanted to forget it.

The elders were sitting in the throne-like chairs when they came out. Raynor approached Bhaskar first, took the outstretched hand offered him and touched his forehead to it. Then, he did the same with the other two. It looked archaic to her and extremely respectful.

Following his lead, Briana touched her forehead to each of the elder's hands. "We are glad you found your way back to us, my child," Gorna said gently, caressing her cheek after she finished her farewell exchange. The other two nodded their heads in solemn agreement.

When they turned to leave, Bhaskar called after them, "Bring your children to see us."

Raynor said they would, and then held her hand while they started the long trek down the winding tunnels.

She burst the quiet of the trek with an anxious question, "Raynor, I have to know what the elders told you about the snakewoman."

Stopping, he looked at her, a lovely smile lighting his face. "How do you know they told me anything?"

Shrugging, she chewed her bottom lip. "I don' t, I just hoped you were as curious as me and asked."

Laughter shook his broad shoulders. "You were right, I did."

"And?" Irritation edged her voice.

"Nothing to worry about, my love." He placed one hand along her cheek and stared into her eyes. "They said the memory of the snake goddess is fuzzy, because only one of our ancestors ever ran across her."

She frowned, awaiting further explanation.

"Apparently, according to the memories, she actually was a goddess on her planet, not simply another life form."

"Oh, come on, Raynor, a real goddess!"

He chuckled and nodded his head.

"But, what does it all mean?" Her heart was pounding. Why had she changed into that creature?

"It means that you probably are a direct descendant of that one ancient shifter; thus, your gene memory is stronger."

"Nothing more...I' m not going to change into her here, or be weird, or something?"

"No, Briana." He took her upper arms in his strong hands, making her look up at him. "You will only shift into a werewolf here." He plastered a lopsided grin on his face. "The only other consequence is, if other shifters hear of this—you may develop a fan club."

She groaned, and then grabbed his lower arms, shaking him slightly. "Promise me you won' t tell anyone."

He appeared on the verge of denying her request by the twist of his lips, or perhaps she was in for some intense teasing, but then he seemed to consider her expression seriously.

"Never, not unless you told me to."

She sighed.

"Of course, it might be hard, getting used to living with a goddess."

Briana punched him in the ribs. He just couldn' t resist teasing her. "If she were a goddess, don' t you think she' d have some special powers — like maybe shooting rays from her eyes or something?"

A wide grin flitted across his face. "One would think so, the elders certainly thought so."

Stopping in her tracks, she stared at him with surprise. "Then why didn't I have any of those powers when I could have used them?"

Raynor rubbed his chin. "Perhaps because you are untrained, or maybe some part of you, that is Briana, didn' t want to let loose such powers."

She was lost in thought. What would have happened if she'd had her full powers as Raynor suggested? Would she have blasted the vampires into cinders with one look? "You're probably right." Laughing softly, she remarked, "It's just as well. She did enough damage without super snakewoman abilities."

The next minute she asked, "But what was all that talk about the old gods?"

"It's a superstition...legend, if you will, among shapeshifters." Raynor's look turned inward, as if searching for her answer. "Remember how I explained that the snakewoman is a gene memory from an actual snake goddess?"

She nodded, intrigued.

"There are a few shapeshifters who are rarely seen, even among our people, such as the snake goddess. And all such creatures have been gods or goddesses on their home planets, with vast powers at their disposal."

"Like...what other kinds?" She was almost afraid to ask, but couldn't seem to help herself.

He furrowed his brow. "Oh, there's the worm god."

"Sounds yucky," she shuddered. "Is it huge and ugly?"

"Ugly, but about this size." Raynor measured a hand span with his palms. He chuckled at her look. "Don't knock the little guy, his powers are tremendous."

"I'm sure. Any gods or goddesses less repugnant?"

"Hmm, there's the tigress goddess—very beautiful and very deadly."

She sighed. "So, I' m in good company, then?" Her tone conveyed anything but respect.

"Better than you could know."

His smile reassured her a touch. The next minute her thoughts turned one hundred and eighty degrees and she asked anxiously, "What about Robert?"

"They didn't tell me, but I got a psychic impression from them, his murder was not fated."

Stopping suddenly, she grabbed his hands in excitement. "Do you think they'll send someone back to correct it?"

Nodding, he said, "I believe they will." He tugged on her hand, and they walked onward.

After a few minutes, she couldn' t stand it any longer, and asked, "Where are we going?"

He stopped and looked at her with humor. "Home."

"But, whose home, yours or mine?"

Cocking his head, he smiled. "Are you completely content, my love, in your home and job?"

She shrugged, a frisson of surprise flushing through her, but she shouldn't be caught off guard by now. Many times Raynor seemed to know much about her that never was spoken. Her job had become too stressful this last year, the boss giving her more and more responsibility without financial compensation. Many of the maids and other staff were lazy and had to be constantly monitored. And the traffic in Dallas was horrific around the loop, had been for years. Oftentimes, she'd dreamed of escaping to a smaller city and living out her life in a simpler life style.

"I've always wanted to live in…" She paused and giggled. "Where do you live?" She couldn't help teasing him; of course she remembered his hometown.

"Phoenix."

"I've always wanted to live in Phoenix."

"Is that right?" He placed his strong arms about her and rubbed his nose against hers.

"Wait a minute, I was just thinking I was tired of the big city life. Isn't Phoenix larger than Dallas?"

"Actually, I live in a big old ranch house outside Phoenix."

"Do you ranch? What happened to gym manager?"

He chucked her under the chin. "The only thing you could ranch around my house is lizards and snakes." At her disapproving look, he said, "There's barely an acre around the house. I drive in to work at the gym, which luckily is located on the border of Phoenix." He put his arms around her. "You'll like it. The peace, only insects singing at night, and the stars…there's a whole sky full."

"You talk like a romantic." She smiled.

"Haven't I been trying to convince you of that all along?"

"Why, sir, you're a virtual knight…you just didn't dress like one." His frown was foiled by the merry twinkling in his amber eyes.

Her thoughts went back to his home. A ranch...how quaint and welcome it sounded. Suddenly she was so very glad she had always been curious about Phoenix. She spoke into the contented silence between them, "But first I'd like to finish my vacation, if you can come with me?"

A wary expression flickered through his eyes. "What were you doing on your vacation?"

"Oh, let's see, there was yoga, mud baths, and of course learning to make pottery out of clay." She had to giggle at his stricken look. "There are also nature trails to hike beside a lovely river, natural hot tub pools, and a cozy hotel room with a very comfy bed just waiting to be 'slept' in."

Raynor grinned. "Now you're speaking my language."

They smiled at one another, and holding hands, while they proceeded toward the entrance. It took only a few more minutes to reach the opening to the cave, or the exit this time. They stepped through and the odd sensation of nausea ran through her system again. "Raynor, how do the elders keep humans from finding the entrance?"

"Remember, they cast a magic shield. Any human who gets close to it, sees a solid cliff. Only shifters can see the opening." He ran one hand up and down the cliff wall.

"What if a human being accidentally fell against the opening?"

"Samething. They'd feel a rock face."

Unexpectedly, they heard noise below them. Peering over the ledge, they saw four people climbing upward, a man, woman, and two boys.

"Are they shifters?" She whispered.

Raynor sniffed the air. "Nope, human."

"Hello," the man greeted them in a friendly way. The woman smiled and the two energetic boys ran past them to perch on the ledge's edge.

"Get down from there," the woman said nervously.

"Listen to your mother," the man said firmly.

Grumbling the boys climbed down and began to throw rocks off the cliff edge.

"Kids," the man shrugged and they smiled back. The stranger turned and surveyed his surroundings. "You know, I told my wife, I didn't know if this climb would be worth it, but it's a pretty spectacular view."

"Yes, it is." Raynor answered.

"Hey," one of the boys pointed upward. "Look the moon's full."

Everyone looked up. It was several hours before sunset, but the moon had risen already, its pale spherical shape lovely against the dark blue sky.

The same boy growled, made awful faces at his brother, and then yelled, "Watch out, the werewolf's gonna get you."

The younger boy screamed and then the next instant the two were tussling on the ground.

"Boys," the father sighed and walked over to break up the fight.

Briana giggled, and they waved goodbye when they started down the trail. Stopping on a much smaller ledge later for a breather, Raynor unexpectedly asked, "So, did you ever decide?"

"Huh? What?"

"If you love me or just kind of do?" His voice was definitely teasing.

"I've decided I'm head over heels in love."

His expression turn heated when he growled, "Better watch out for the werewolf tonight."

She hugged his body to hers in a tight embrace. "Oh, I certainly hope so." His amber eyes flashed a fiery red for a second and she shivered in anticipation.

Enjoy this excerpt from
AS YOU WISH
© Copyright Myra Nour 2004

Once upon a time, long ago in a land far, far away, there was born a girl of extraordinary beauty. Her parents named her Amira, meaning Queen, because she was so lovely and they hoped her future would shine as brightly as her physical appearance.

Fate was not as kind to the fair maiden as her parents had prayed. Her silken, gold hair, delicate face, and slender form drew the attention of not only those who truly loved her, but the unwanted attention of a powerful, evil sorcerer. The wizard Bakr desired the fair maiden and wooed Amira with words plucked from a dead poet' s heart, and the finest silk woven by spiders, creatures created with his magic. His final gift was a breathtakingly beautiful rose carved by trolls from blood-red rubies dug from the Earth's belly.

Alas, the fair maiden was in love with a handsome youth named Omar. Being kind in spirit, Amira turned Bakr down gently, but a scorned sorcerer is not to be reckoned with, and the earth trembled as the wizard's anger spewed forth violently.

Bakr strove to create a unique and cruel punishment for the fair Amira, turning her into one of the djinn. She would not be an ordinary djinn, like those who granted three wishes of a new Master, moving on to a new owner each time they were fulfilled. Amira would be forever condemned to stay with a Master throughout his lifetime, fulfilling his or her deepest, darkest sexual desires.

Every djinn is governed by rules, set forth by the Master djinn, Hadji. A powerful sorcerer may succeed in changing the edicts slightly, as Bakr did, adding one specifically tortuous command. Amira was compelled to watch the fulfillment of her Masters' sexual desires while she was forever denied physical release, unless it came by her own hand.

Throughout the endless centuries, Amira lived alone in her lamp, serving countless self-centered Masters, and long ago *sickened by their lustful, selfish fantasies. Oftentimes, sorrow overcame her and she dared to dream of the day a caring Master would release her from eternal imprisonment. The fair maiden wept through the centuries and millennia, her tears sparkling like splintering diamonds dropped from a dragon' s eye. Would any Master ever fulfill her wish?*

"So…you grant me three wishes?"

"No," she shook her head, sending her silken ponytail swishing back and forth. "I grant your wishes as long as you are my Master."

"Really?" Nick rubbed his chin. "This is starting to look up." Staring at her lush curves, his thoughts flew here and there. "All right, I wish for a million dollars." He tapped the palm of one hand. "Right here."

"Oh, I' m sorry, Master. I can only grant certain kinds of wishes."

"Wait a minute, you're setting conditions. I thought I was the Master," he chuckled.

"You are." She executed a graceful bow of her head and upper body. "But I am restricted by rules."

Folding his arms, Nick stared at her. "This sounds fishy, but go ahead, give me the bad news. You' re probably going to tell me I can only use my wishes for the good of mankind, or maybe I can' t wish for things like material gains."

The genie sighed softly. "I wish that were so, Master. I can only grant your sexual desires."

"My sexual wishes?" Nick stared hard at her. Was she serious?

"Yes." Her lovely face was totally serious.

As he leaned back into the couch, Nick's arms gripped his body tight in a self-hug. Congratulatory. She could grant a life-long dream come true? "You're not kidding, are you?"

She shook her head in the negative.

"Anything I wish sexually?"

"Yes," she whispered.

Man, how many of his hot dreams as a youth had been filled with imagining a genie at his disposal? Lots.

Nick's mind was a whirl of possibilities. Any sexual desire? He had so many. He had already managed to fulfill sexual fantasies many men only dreamed of, but still, there had to be some that were out of even his reach. His thoughts latched onto the potential. Finally, his mind was spinning with so many erotic images he had to take a break.

Shaking himself mentally, Nick zoomed in on the very bizarre reality of a genie standing patiently, awaiting his sexual desires. He realized she was the most beautiful woman he'd ever laid eyes on, and he'd known plenty. Those amber eyes matched perfectly with the golden hair that caressed the slender waist. Even her skin matched, with its golden-brown glow. She was a golden goddess.

Suddenly, he knew what he wanted. He wanted to see his genie naked. See if the curls covering her pussy were as golden as the rest of her. He wanted her.

Going up and down her form with his eyes, he could find no fault with the firm, round breasts that were exposed above the low cut bodice of the pearl-trimmed harem top. Her curving waist flared into womanly hips, and he bet her butt was as inviting as her breasts.

Finally his eyes came up to her golden ones. "My wish is to fuck you."

About the author:

Myra Nour grew up reading s/f, fantasy, and romance, so she was really thrilled when these elements were combined in Futuristic Romances. She enjoys writing within all these elements, whether the hero is a handsome man from another planet, or a tiny fairy from another dimension. Myra's background is in counseling, and she likes using her knowledge to create believable characters. She also enjoys lively dialogue and, of course, using her imagination to create other worlds with lots of action/adventure, as well as romance. She uses her handsome husband as inspiration for her heroes - he is a body builder, a soldier, and has a black belt in Tae Kwon Do.

Myra welcomes mail from readers. You can write to her c/o Ellora's Cave Publishing at 1337 Commerce Drive, Suite 13, Stow OH 44224.

Why an electronic book?

We live in the Information Age — an exciting time in the history of human civilization in which technology rules supreme and continues to progress in leaps and bounds every minute of every hour of every day. For a multitude of reasons, more and more avid literary fans are opting to purchase e-books instead of paperbacks. The question to those not yet initiated to the world of electronic reading is simply: *why?*

1. *Price.* An electronic title at Ellora' s Cave Publishing runs anywhere from 40-75% less than the cover price of the <u>exact same title</u> in paperback format. Why? Cold mathematics. It is less expensive to publish an e-book than it is to publish a paperback, so the savings are passed along to the consumer.

2. *Space.* Running out of room to house your paperback books? That is one worry you will never have with electronic novels. For a low one-time cost, you can purchase a handheld computer designed specifically for e-reading purposes. Many e-readers are larger than the average handheld, giving you plenty of screen room. Better yet, hundreds of titles can be stored within your new library — a single microchip. (Please note that Ellora' s Cave does not endorse any specific brands. You can check our website at www.ellorascave.com for customer recommendations we make available to new consumers.)

3. *Mobility*. Because your new library now consists of only a microchip, your entire cache of books can be taken with you wherever you go.

4. *Personal preferences are accounted for*. Are the words you are currently reading too small? Too large? Too...**ANNOYING**? Paperback books cannot be modified according to personal preferences, but e-books can.

5. *Innovation*. The way you read a book is not the only advancement the Information Age has gifted the literary community with. There is also the factor of what you can read. Ellora' s Cave Publishing will be introducing a new line of interactive titles that are available in e-book format only.

6. *Instant gratification*. Is it the middle of the night and all the bookstores are closed? Are you tired of waiting days—sometimes weeks—for online and offline bookstores to ship the novels you bought? Ellora' s Cave Publishing sells instantaneous downloads 24 hours a day, 7 days a week, 365 days a year. Our e-book delivery system is 100% automated, meaning your order is filled as soon as you pay for it.

Those are a few of the top reasons why electronic novels are displacing paperbacks for many an avid reader. As always, Ellora' s Cave Publishing welcomes your questions and comments. We invite you to email us at service@ellorascave.com or write to us directly at: 1337 Commerce Drive, Suite 13, Stow OH 44224.

Discover for yourself why readers can' t get enough of the multiple award-winning publisher Ellora' s Cave. Whether you prefer e-books or paperbacks, be sure to visit EC on the web at www.ellorascave.com for an erotic reading experience that will leave you breathless.

Printed in the United States
25755LVS00004B/67-708